Small Hearts

A Story by

Bryan W. Dull

Illustrations by Alexis Dull
Published by Athropolis Publishing
Text Copyright © 2020, 2019 Bryan W. Dull

This is a work of fiction. All characters and events portrayed in this novel are fictitious and are products of the author's imagination. Any resemblance to actual events, locales or persons, is purely coincidental.

"It is under the greatest adversity that there exists the greatest potential for doing good, both for oneself and others."

— Dalai Lama XIV

Author's Note

I am ashamed of myself.

The fact that this story even entered my mind is disgusting, even by my standards. Even so, it is a story that is worth telling in the long run. We sit back and watch events unfold in the news regarding the violence we inflict on ourselves only to get on our social media high horse. We tell others how we are praying for the families of those involved. We really mean that we want others to acknowledge us with "likes" and "favorites" on our feed in our false sense of reality. To feel special for a paltry minute while the actual people involved could care less about our "prayers." They are too busy reaching for a light, a glimmer of hope that may never come to them.

Nevertheless, some stories are worth telling, regardless if they are fiction or not. The events in this book are not real in the strictest sense, but most fiction is based in some reality, and this is the closest home that I may ever get to in this writing endeavor. The difference is that my discomfort in writing this book is trivial compared to the reality that others have faced. When I get done writing for the night, I can play a game or even go to bed. I'm not here to preach to you about social events, government, politics, or anything else. Just realize that what happens in this book could have been or was someone else's reality. We will never fathom what it was like those tragic days in our history as the victims' friends and families. We will uncontrollably wonder what their loved ones' final moments were like as they cry to themselves at night. While the rest of us have unwittingly forgotten and moved on, we unknowingly wait for the next tragedy to occur as history repeats itself. Instead of years, it's now only a matter of days.

I realize that this novel will be off-putting for some based on the way it is structured. No one likes thinking about the events that unfurl in this novel. You need to know that I am trying not to focus on the bad as I attempt to show off parts of the characters' lives and how some individuals can affect others.

For Tammi Renae Dull

(1976 – 2019)

I should have learned more

sign language, but I learned from you the

little bit I know.

The Jagged Dreamscape

She didn't know it, but every time Emily fell asleep, the further away she slipped away from the world she once knew. A few weeks prior, it was hard for her to fall asleep after the incident simply, and no one would blame her due to the atrocity that occurred. Most would say that it was a good thing she began to sleep again, but the more she closed her eyes, the harder they were to open.

Emily dreamt of a world with a wooded area with a long dirt path surrounded by trees that grew with purple leaves and a red sky that illuminated this strange reality. She walked the way that ended abruptly where the ground changed from brown to black, reminding her of charcoal. Emily looked above her and saw the sky turn pink with white clouds as the dirt emitted small, blue orbs of light. She ran to it each time she dreamt about it, but the path just stretched out even further like the dream itself didn't want her to reach it; there was no end, ever. The truth was that she didn't want to wake up. Running down that path that ultimately got her nowhere was a better option than going back to the memories, the horror, and what followed her in the real world. She just wanted to sleep it away, but she couldn't. Emily needed to deal with the ghosts that haunted her in her visions and life.

However, Emily was tired. The nightmare she lived, both in and out of consciousness, was exhausting. If her stalkers were going to be the end of her, she wished that it would hurry and just happen instead of the torturing her psyche was experiencing. Tonight's dream was the last of her running. As she lay on the black, ash-like ground, Emily decided that she could not escape her reality any longer. She curled herself into a ball, naked and alone in the forest of her dreams underneath the bloodshot red sky; she preferred the pink as it was not as intimidating. The atmosphere opened above her, and it began to rain, making the ground like sludge. Emily's body began to sink into the ground.

This is it, she thought, forgetting that she was dreaming. *This is how I repent. This is my sentence and my salvation all at once.*

The rain fell onto her body. Every drop that cascading down her olive-colored skin turned it gray, becoming almost as dark as the ground that was consuming her. Half of her body had sunk into the soil of the strange world. A world that she had visited in her mind many times before. *Would I still have seen this place if the children...if what happened didn't occur?*

Many questions came to her mind over the nights she did sleep these past few weeks. However, Emily was too exhausted to find the answers. As Emily sank into the dirt and the darkness, she felt a calm wash over her. There was nothing now—no nightmare, no joy, no beauty—and Emily was content with that. Before the ground engulfed her, her body began to rise. Hands from beneath her had emerged through the black soil. They pushed underneath Emily's body from underneath, straining to place her above the land again. Emily heard the moans of others beneath her as they shoved their cold hands against her sides. It wasn't just one set of hands. She began to feel six, *no wait,* around eight hands on her body. *No! This isn't what I want! Leave me alone! I just want to die!* The sounds of tortured souls began to wail louder, saddened by Emily's resolve to perish in her dream. For Emily, dying in her jagged and somber dreamscape was not enough as she wondered if there was still a point in existing at all.

Emily heard the echoes of tiny voices, recognizing every one of them. She felt their small hands pushing as hard as they could through the muck, even when Emily pleaded for them to stop. Those little hands, those tiny voices, those small hearts, brought her to the surface. When Emily stood on her two feet again, Emily looked down to see their fingers disappear back into the black dirt. Whispers filled her mind with the sounds of little boys and girls she once knew. *It's okay. We are fine. Don't worry about us. We will be all right. You don't need to be here anymore. Go and be happy.* Emily cried, and as her tears poured down her face, her skin tone and complexion returned to their olive color. As much as she had lost hope, her tears proved there was still life in her. Bellowing into the red sky as Emily fell onto her bare knees, Emily's tears fell from her chin, landing on the black soil. The world began to turn the land around her green as the grass grew as she soaked in her sadness; it seemed full of life now. There was life in this drab dreamscape, but something was fighting against the light.

"Your fault," a dark, menacing voice said from the trees beside her. Emily could see a set of glowing orange eyes in the distance. Emily stood naked, cold, and scared. As she began to walk away from what she thought was a monster, a person, hunched over and in pain, crawled out of the shrubbery, scuttling slowly toward Emily. Emily squinted her eyes to recognize who or what was close. It was another woman with wet, dark hair covering her face. The woman yelped in pain as bones popped out of sockets as she came closer to Emily. She

looked sick with the same aged, discolored skin that Emily had after the rain washed over her. The person looked up at Emily with her round, glowing orange eyes.

She's not a monster, Emily thought to herself as she realized, *She's me!*

The creature's gums and teeth began to grow outside its mouth to catch and engulf Emily's body. The beast drew closer and closer to Emily, shaking and shaking its head back and forth, spattering saliva onto Emily's back. The droll was warm and felt like thick plasm running down her torso. The ooze spread, beginning to envelop parts of her and eventually reaching her legs, hardening like concrete. Emily's legs fought hard to move, but she could no longer run. Emily again fell to the ground, flipping onto her back, defending herself from this creature, a demon—this other version of her.

There was no way for Emily to defend herself now. The demon creature placed its front claws over her hands and inched toward her face with a hot, putrid breath. The creature's face began to morph back into a replica of Emily's as its sharp claws transformed into human hands. They went from trapping Emily's hands to holding them as a loved one would. Straddling Emily, the dark version of herself leaned in, stared her in the eyes, and whispered, "*Accept it. You failed, and there is nothing you can do to take it back.*"

The creature's mouth twitched, splitting apart into four quadrants with razor-sharp teeth piercing through its gums. Emily thought she was going to die in her dream of being swallowed whole. It was just a dream, but it was becoming increasingly difficult for her to wake up. It wouldn't have been impossible for her to stay asleep this time for good. Emily looked inside the back of its throat, waiting for the inevitable feast that she would become. Suddenly, a large tongue shot out of the creature's mouth. Like a tentacle, it grasped Emily's neck and held her in place with the suckers on its tongue as its mouth squirmed closer to her face. Emily could hear the children in her life that had suddenly disappeared into the real world as the creature was consuming her head. They were talking to one another, asking questions; *Why are you here? It's okay! Wake up!*

Emily's eyes shot open as she woke from the nightmare. Gasping for air, she kept her eyes fixated on the ceiling. *Jesus!* She whispered to herself. For the last three weeks, Emily had been alone in her apartment. It seemed like the world was leaving her behind with every day that passed. She was lonely, and the only events that acknowledged her were the visions she was seeing—the ghosts that kept following her. Emily just wanted to go away, either from life or just from the town she once loved.

It was four o'clock in the afternoon when she awoke. The shades were closed, making it seem like the middle of the night because the days were becoming shorter in the fall. Emily had to get up. *Get up!* Emily knew that deep down, she needed to find someone to talk to, if only for a day. *Hell. Just an hour would be fine.* The school system she worked for had an assistance program for her to find a psychiatrist to talk to, all expenses paid. The idea of spending a hundred dollars per hour to speak to a stranger made her body clench up. She had to do it regardless if she ever wanted to teach in her school district again.

The air felt thick; it was hard to breathe. Emily felt weighed down. When she went to move her arms and legs a little, it was more of a burden than it should have been. She raised her head a bit to see the end of her bed. A small, gray-skinned child, eyes filled with blackness, stared at her from the foot of the bed as he sat Indian-style on the end of the mattress, staring at her. *Wait. It's hard to move my arms as well.* Moving her head, Emily looked to her left and right quickly; she saw four more children, two boys and two girls. Looking down at her with the same dark eyes, the kids sat on the comforter on both sides of the bed, trapping Emily's arms and hands underneath were engulfed in darkness.

As hard as it was for her to move, Emily sat up in the bed. She bent her knees up to her chest, pushing her body against the headboard behind her, scared. She looked around her bed and room to count seven ghostly children surrounding her. One of them ran up to the bed from the bathroom, scaring Emily.

"What do you want? Leave me alone!" Emily screamed. As she cried and pleaded, the gray children opened their mouths, and all began to bawl together. The sound of their cries broke Emily's heart, and the more she wept, the louder the ghosts cried. Their melancholy moans echoed through the room, and all Emily could do was put her hands over her ears and wish it to go away.

"I'm sorry," she whispered, "I'm sorry about what happened to you, but it's not my fault that you died!" At least that is what she told herself.

You Can Eat Soup Off the Floor

No one ever tells you when you get older that some of the things that you hold dear in life will change at the drop of a dime. For some, it comes with the realization that your parents aren't the people that you thought they were. Parents are flawed human beings, just like anyone else you meet. Your ideologies eventually clash, and arguments begin about topics that don't matter at the end of the day. One day a girl brings home a boyfriend of another ethnicity, and she then finds that her father, a man she loves and has always respected, is a bigot. How do you deal with that? There is usually an event that forces us to live or mature sooner than we anticipated.

Parents tell you that you can be anything you want to be when you get older, but you can't. More times than not, these truths are realized at some point. In a perfect world, sure, you can, with hard work and determination. For others, though, they don't get that option. Some grow up poor and live in an area where their dreams don't come to fruition as college costs rise and poverty increases. Occasionally, an individual will chart out a plan to get out of the place that tried to hold them back by saving money from the time they are in high school. Emily Sinclair was a rare person who got out and made a name for herself. She moved away from her parents' overbearing force with their 'do what I say and make us happy attitude.' It was this narcissistic nature that Emily found to be true later in her life. She was not her parents, and she would prove it, not to others, but herself.

Emily's social status over the years was not lost on her. She came from a family that never pushed for college. She never thought of her or her family as "well off." The Sinclair family did well for themselves and achieved the "American Dream," as described by the Baby Boomers. They had a house, kids, a dog, and perhaps a white picket fence. Her mother was the stay-at-home type who loved to spend the money she was not earning. Emily had most of those things except for the fence.

Her father was a man who despised school and worked on his own to climb the corporate ladder without paying tuition for two to four years. The issue was that most employers require that piece of paper that now costs thousands of dollars to obtain. Emily knew this, played it smart, and went on to college despite the cost and risking her father's disapproval as he *didn't need it in his life, so why should she?*

As a Notre Dame graduate, Emily chose to take her degree in teaching and work, where she felt it would count the most. She put her sights toward Cincinnati, Ohio. Emily moved there after finding an apartment above a corner consignment shop in the Marie-Glen township. The county's visual and moral opposite grew up in South Carolina, where people were taught and savored ignorance because of the misguided bliss it created. Not all, but many thought like that. *If you were not this or that, then you were nothing at all to those people.* That may hold some truth overall, but at least people could have been nicer about it instead of telling others that you would burn in Hell. At least that's what Emily thought.

Marie-Glen was a small area located off one of the major highways in Cincinnati. It was one of the most sought-after places to live because of its rustic aesthetic. The German cottages used as local businesses close to the local mall without traffic made it ideal. Cincinnati's public education was in trouble as programs were systematically being removed from the curriculum. The decision to cut art and music classes boggled

Emily as she heard about the problems she may have to face. In a world where most of the things we take for granted in schools, like the arts, were taken away without a second thought. Emily Sinclair was determined to get through it until things got better. The only way to do that was to play the bureaucratic game of aiding, helping kids improve their scores so the county could get more funding. *You must get excellent grades to be able to get more excellent grades through funding? That's some bullshit.* Of course, she couldn't do it alone. Emily was the go-getter of the family. If there was anything she could do, she could entice people to follow her lead.

Emily Sinclair was the teacher that others aspired to be and what older educators wished they were. In the two years, she did this at Marie-Glen Elementary as a third-grade teacher and then a fourth-grade teacher. No one ever tells you when you get older that some of the things that you hold dear in life will change at the drop of a dime. It wasn't a realization about her parents not being perfect or people being awful to one another. On the fifteenth of October, it was the sound of a shotgun fired in the hallways of Marie-Glen Elementary that altered Emily's life.

Emily didn't know why she was standing in front of a blue door attached to a doctor's office. The past took over her mind for a moment as gunfire echoed within. She shook her head slightly and came back to reality.

She was a strong-willed, bullheaded person who had to admit that she needed to walk into the psychologist's office. Her father would have told her seeing a shrink was a trait of weakness, but just like most things involving him, she took pleasure in doing the opposite. There was more than a moment of hesitation as she held a piece of yellow office paper with the address scribbled on it. The fall colors flew past her face and body as leaves shuffled in the wind, and all she could think about was the beautiful brick exterior of the building.

The township of Marie-Glen was nothing like she had ever encountered before. It was like walking around a piece of history where nothing had changed except for the people who occupied it. The brick roads and the stoplights that stood on the street corners accentuated this. Typically, they hung above the streets, but not in this township. Marie-Glen was not a big area in comparison to other towns within Cincinnati. If you didn't pay attention, you could leave it without realizing that you had passed it after a few stoplights on Main Street. The town square consisted of various shops. There were independently owned places, a couple of chain restaurants. The highlight was a theater that would show films the mainstream had never heard of, instead of the latest action flick that starred famous actors contracted for multiple sequels.

This is it, Emily," she whispered to herself, *"you crazy chick you,* she whispered to herself.

In the middle of the beauty surrounding her, there was consistent darkness lurking. Something, or someone, was stalking her. That was a lie that Emily told herself. She was convinced, no, she knew there was more than one.

She knew they were watching her. Their presence came from the end of the alleyway, where the doctor's office front door was. Her eyes remained ahead as she debated about walking in, but they would make her as they slowly crept towards her. She turned her head, knowing what she would see: a group of pale children with piercing blue eyes and black smoke surrounding them. They had shown up time and time again only to torment Emily since the tragedy. She was sure it was only in her mind, but she had to know for sure. *What if the shrink does indeed tell me I see things?* Emily asked herself frequently. *Then I will be certifiably loony.*

She quickly glanced down the alley to find that she was wrong about the children staring at her down the way. "Maybe I am not crazy," she said as she began to convince herself, justifying not seeing the psychiatrist after all. Emily turned to walk back to the main road and was startled by nine children staring at her with their white hair and blue, dead eyes. Emily, startled, put her hand over her mouth so other people couldn't hear her scream into it. The children didn't see what she did, and they already had an ax to grind with her as far as Emily was concerned. She backed away from the children, reaching for the door that she was afraid to enter moments earlier. They pointed at Emily, opening and closing their mouths like they wanted to say something. At the same time, nothing but dry gasps and clicking sounds from their chattering teeth surrounded her.

"What do you want from me?" she yelled through her hand, silencing her voice. Emily turned around to face the door. The closer her hand got to the doorknob, the closer the ghostly children came toward her. She grabbed the doorknob, and without any restraint, the door flew open. Emily rushed into the room, hiding from the nightmare she had been trying to forget for weeks as this was just one of many of Emily's delusions that had been occurring. Luckily, the shrink that Emily was debating on seeing was already prepared in his office.

2

"Please, come on in," the man wearing a gray cardigan said as he sat up from his worn-in blue, Marmont leather chair. He was attempting to be funny, but instead, he managed to add to Emily's anxiety more as she thought that her barging in had upset the man."

"I'm sorry," she apologized as she looked back at the door to make sure no one else was coming through it. Emily nervously began to explain, or in this case, tweak the truth about why she arrived in the manner she did. "I just thought that someone was following me," she explained as she gripped her purse.

The man in the gray cardigan adjusted his blue tie and smiled. "Oh, I'm sure nobody was stalking you," he said, walking closer to her. "At least, not that you know of."

"What?" Emily gasped, not realizing he was joking.

"I'm kidding," he laughed, "Emily, I presume?"

"Yes," she confirmed as she nodded her head, realizing that she never actually made an appointment. "How did you know that I—" she said before the man chimed in.

"Would you come in today? It's a small township here. I don't have that many appointments," he said with a wry smile. The air had an uneasiness about it, a thickness that Emily could cut with a knife. *That didn't answer my question.*

"Between you and me," he continued, "Most of the Marie-Glen socialites would never admit that they have problems." He leaned toward Emily and jested with a fake British accent, "We wouldn't want people to know that the snoots have issues. That would just ruin their caviar and champagne dreams now, wouldn't it?"

Emily chuckled a bit as the man guided her to the taupe-colored couch that looked like better days...in the 80s.

"There is nothing wrong with you. Everything is better than you think!" Paul exclaimed. Emily's eyes widened as she watched him move to his chair out from his desk.

He saw Emily's glare and told her, "I'm kidding. How would I know that? I just met you."

This man is making me nervous. He doesn't seem like a shrink. He's more like a car salesman that just did a bump of cocaine, Emily thought. Emily sat down and looked at the oak table in front of her. She found that recent magazines were strewn about evenly, with one publication slightly draped over the other, going from largest to smallest. He had the whole spectrum of reading material to appease everyone: Popular Science to Entertainment Weekly. Emily was surprised by this as she had never been in a doctor's office with the most recent issues of magazines before.

"My name is Doctor Paul Cusick, in case you didn't already gather that by the nameplate atop my desk. I will be your psychologist or therapist if you prefer today."

Emily nodded and felt the need to ask a question that she often asked herself. "What is the difference?"

"In what?" Paul asked.

Emily gripped her bag again and got more specific. "Between a psychologist and a psychiatrist. What is the difference? I never bothered to look it up even though I wondered sometimes."

Paul bit the end of his pen, leering at Emily only to smile, and chuckled, "From what I understand, about fifty grand more a year." He laughed at his wit as he leaned into his chair. No one could ever say that Paul Cusick didn't have a sense of humor.

Emily took a moment as Paul giggled to look around his office. She didn't know what to expect, aside from what she saw in the movies. As if someone recently painted, the walls were a light cocoa color, while the trim around the room was a bold shade of white. She would expect a muted color carpet or a dark hardwood floor. She was surprised to see a very light-colored tile floor; Not the small tiles, but the larger tiles that someone would use in a kitchen typically. They were so clean that Emily could see the reflection of the furniture and the lights above.

Paul Cusick's office was a bit of an enigma. It was one giant room with minimalistic decorating, and the only door was the blue door she entered through. *Where did he use the bathroom?* Emily wondered.

Paul noticed Emily's eyes scanning the room. Immediately he asked, "What do you think of the office?"

"To be honest, it's not what I thought it would be," she replied, "I just had it different in my head."

"How so?" Paul asked.

Emily put her pointer finger to her lip to concentrate on what was bothering her about the room. "I guess it's just decorated differently," she said, "I mean, I don't mean to put in a cliché, but—"

"—it doesn't look like an L.L. Bean catalog," he finished her sentence.

Emily sighed and nervously gasped, "Yeah!" with a sound of relief, knowing she wasn't offensive.

Paul snickered and explained, "I think you will find, Emily, that I don't do things normally than how us shrinks are stereotyped. Hopefully, you find more peace after our session with my methods."

Emily nodded and retorted, "I don't know if you can. I think I may be more of a subject that is above your pay grade."

Paul smiled slyly and said, "We'll see. Just know you are not a subject. You are a human being."

Looking back at the floors near the window facing the back of the building, Emily was still in awe of the floor's cleanliness. Not even the dirt she would have dragged in showed up. "Who is your cleaning service?" she asked Paul. "I mean, you could eat soup off this fl...."

Emily looked at the reflection of the window in the tile just as she was finishing her sentence. With their piercing blue eyes engulfed in black, the ghostly children stared at her through the window. She could only see them in the reflection of the clean floor under her. When Emily raised her eyes to the actual window, nothing was there. She looked back down, and the children pointed at her upside down with their unsettling moans and clicking, chattering teeth. Putting her hands over her eyes, she lightly yelped.

Paul tilted his head and looked at the same window knowing that Emily thought she had seen something. "Emily," he sighed with genuine worry, "How can I help you?"

3

"I see them," she whispered as her eyes moved around the room., "They show up surrounding me, pointing, yelling at me. Looking through me with their dead eyes."

Paul was not surprised by this as he already knew the circumstances of her visit. Putting away his humor, Paul leaned in and asked, "Can you tell me everything that has happened? Will you tell me what you see?"

Hunched over, sniffling, Emily slid her hands down from her eyes and placed her chin on her palms as she rested her elbows on her legs. "Every time I see them, they have these blue, dead eyes. Not all of them, though. The ones that scare me the most are the ones with lights inside them."

Paul sat back in his chair and inquired, "What did you see just then?"

"The ones with dark, dead eyes with the blue in the middle. They were in the reflection of the window on your tile."

Paul still didn't appear to seem surprised by the answer and pressed on.

"Why there? Why not just show up in the window normally?"

"They hide; when others are around, they hide?" Emily said, unsure, paranoid by knowing how crazy she sounded.

Fortunately for her, Paul had had significant practice with this type of patient and this situation.

"Do they touch you?" he asked as he unleashed questions. "Do they move things? Do you hear or see them opening or closing windows? Do you see them slamming doors?"

Emily's tears ran down her face and into her hands that were holding it. She had dreaded this part for a while now, but it was too late to turn back. The children that haunted her were becoming relentless, and there was no escape at this point as Paul's office may be the last safe place for her now. Her only hope was for Paul to bring her back to what she hoped was reality and try to forget the tragedy that happened a month before.

"All I know is that every time they come closer to me, a piece of myself goes away. The part that scares me most is that I think I like it."

Paul began to write in his notepad. Emily knew that this would happen; she had to accept it as he studied her like a monkey.

"Do they seem that real? Are they afraid of you at all?"

"No. Not at all. None of them are afraid. They have no reason to be," Emily replied. Seemingly confused from Emily's perspective, Paul simply asked, "Why?"

"Isn't it obvious?" she calmly said, "They were kids that I once knew."

The First Day of Class

About two years ago, on a Thursday at 6:30 in the morning, Emily Sinclair got the call to meet with Marie-Glen's Elementary dean, Dean Williams. That was his actual name. Every time Emily thought about that, she chuckled to herself; *It was like his career was already chosen for him; it was meant to be with a name like that.*

Emily's cell phone ring was the sound of the ocean crashing. There had never been a time when she answered someone's call the first time because it was so quiet, even on the highest volume setting. Her fiancé, Crosby Fulton, was the opposite as he preferred the louder noises to fall asleep. After a few months of being together, Emily had enough of the grunge rock music playing while she attempted to sleep. Crosby would play an entire Stone Temple Pilots album, and that was enough to knock him out. Still, after Emily bogged him down with endless gripes, he finally agreed to put on headphones when he went to bed.

Whoosh…. whooooooosh. Emily's cell phone went off, and the first to hear it was Crosby. For a person needing loud music to go to sleep, the smallest noises woke him up. "Your phone is ringing," he said, annoyed, mumbling into the stained pillow from the mix of toothpaste and drool. Emily moaned and grumbled her way out of bed. There was no doubt, in Emily's mind, this was a call to substitute a class.

For the past few months since the beginning of the previous school year, Emily worked substituting for the school with the board's promise that the next opening would be hers. The turnover in staff was almost nonexistent at Marie-Glen Elementary. Hell, it was almost like an act of Congress just to get an interview there. The town elementary school was not a typical public school. There had been several occasions where it was awarded multiple times for the caliber of grades. Many students that came from there in the past thrived as they got older. It was also a place that made the teachers accountable for the children's performance and behavior.

Shuffling out of bed, Emily grabbed her phone, charging on her dresser. She picked her underwear out of the crack of her behind. Her brown hair was messy and what she would call 'a rat's nest.'. "Hello," Emily answered, trying to sound upbeat. A string of saliva connected Emily's mouth to her retainer as she pulled it from her mouth.

"Ms. Sinclair! It's Dean Williams!" *He is unusually cheery this morning. Maybe he got laid, or his coffee may have had multiple shots of espresso in it.* "I need you to come down to my office a couple of hours before school starts. I have something I want to talk to you about."

It took a moment for Emily to grasp the nature of to what the Dean of Students may be referring. Her eyes got big, and her attitude changed when she realized that she might be getting a promotion of sorts.

"Absolutely!" she exclaimed, "I'll be there in about thirty minutes!" She hung up the phone, not realizing that she did not say "goodbye" or "see ya later." Emily hopped on the bed and bounced up and down on her knees to wake up Crosby. It was one of her quirks that most would find annoying, but to Crosby, it was endearing... most of the time. "Sweet Jesus, what!"

"Do you know who that was?" she asked.

Crosby sighed, pulled up the comforter, and replied, "I'm not a genius, but I am going to say that it was your boss. The guy you described as a condescending jackass, that guy?" Crosby had a flair for sarcasm.

"I think I may get a full-time position today," Emily exclaimed.

Crosby patted the bed to indicate that he wanted her to lay down next to him. He watched her slide back into bed, looking into her green eyes that he referred to as her 'sparkly jades.' Emily got under the comforter and nudged her backside against him.

"I hope that's true, babe. I just don't want you to get your hopes up too high like you tend to do." He put his fingers through her hair only to get caught in the tangles in which he tried to pull out gently, only to yank her head back a bit.

"When do I do that?" she scoffed.

"Like, I don't know, all the time," Crosby replied, "The time you thought that you were a shoo-in for the free trip to the Bahamas. You know, from that potato chip company because you filled out a thousand entry forms." Emily huffed and annoyingly explained what seemed to be the hundredth time, "They said I could enter as many times as I wanted. The rules were right there on the bag!"

When she looked back on it, there had been many times that she got her hopes up too high. There was the time her grandmother died, and she was confident that she was going to get willed a painting…that never happened. Or when she bought half the roll of lottery scratch-offs just knowing that she would get her money back and then some. That didn't happen either. Emily was the southern version of Clark Griswold that consistently built up grand ideas in her mind that ultimately fell through and disappointed her. "Well, I think it will be. I think there is a perfect shot," she suddenly declared. She turned around to face her love with a hint of playfulness in her eyes. After a few moments, there was a comfortable silence between them, and then Crosby spoke.

"So," he wondered, "since you're up, do you want to raw dog it really quick?"

Emily pushed herself away from his sexual advance. "Ew, Crosby," she exclaimed with a hint of laughter, "Raw-dogging it? Really?" Emily took her pillow and threw it at Crosby, where it landed on his face.

Muffled, Crosby said, "So are you going to take a rain check on that?" Crosby watched her get ready in the bathroom. There was a process for Emily to get prettied up: straighten the brown hair while using the other hand to put on makeup. Not too much, just enough because Emily didn't need it. Then came the careful application of the expensive lip balm with the ingredients to make them look bigger. Emily never viewed herself as having many physical flaws, not because she was conceited. Still, she rarely looked at herself negatively; however, her lips always made her self-conscious. The hyaluronic acid gave her the boost she wanted.

Crosby sat up in the bed and watched her get dressed. As he ran his fingers through his short, sandy blonde hair, he always liked to watch her put pants on because he enjoyed how they went over her ass, and she indeed had one.

Emily walked up to Crosby, kissed him, and with a hint of disgust, blurted, "Brush your damn teeth!" She left the room and then the apartment with a smile, leaving Crosby to his own devices.

2

It's the quiet moments that can be the best for some mental serenity resemblance or the most nerve-wracking. The wall clock in Dean Williams' office was one of the originals installed in Marie-Glen Elementary when built in the early 1980s. The wall clock made a clacking noise every second. Emily sat in the uncomfortable, green pleather chair across from Williams and his obscenely oversized desk in his office. There was a significant silence between them as Emily waited to find out what the conversation would be. Dean Williams looked Emily up and down, sizing her up for the details he was about to speak about, but he was waiting on who would speak first. *Is this a power move?*

Dean Williams wasn't the stereotypical principal or Dean; *whatever else they can be called.* Emily still couldn't figure out why other elementary schools had principals, but Marie-Glen had a dean. The only reason anyone could figure is that the school had an aura of narcissism around it. Emily had always pictured Williams as being the guy who would chain smoke in his office like an advertising executive from the 1960s if it were still allowed.

There wasn't any love lost between Emily and Dean; they were the opposites of what they thought each other should be. Dean wanted his teachers to "drink the Kool-Aid" and be content with anything he, county, or state, said regarding any restrictions forced upon the school. For the last several years, the city of Cincinnati had been cutting back funds for their schools. First, it came in the form of turning off the air conditioning in the spring and summer for hours. Then came the cutting of programs that dealt with the arts; music, drama, and art itself. Then the final straw came when the legal guardians had to start paying for supplies. Books that they would never keep. Supplying pencils, markers, paper, glue, and erasers to keep the classroom stocked for the year. Parents were mainly buying for their kids, but also all the other children in the class.

Unfortunately for Dean, Emily was not a "yes-man" or a "yes-lady" in this case. She had never been one to sit idly by and let thoughts and actions that didn't make sense just go without an objection or a snide remark. She was an enigma in a town that she wanted to live in so badly; she was outspoken while the rest remained conservative within their words.

Phrases that came out of Emily's mouth included, but were not limited to:

"If only closed minds came with closed mouths" and "Your ass must get jealous of all the shit that comes out of your mouth" and other southern quips.

Typically, most would find this to be insubordinate. It was, but Emily had a unique way with children. She had substituted so much that many students would act out if she were not occupying the classroom when their regular teachers were out sick. That and Emily took the gigs at a low pay rate. It meant that she would make a lesser salary than the rest of the tenured teachers because the demand was so low for educators at that point, and Dean Williams knew it.

"Mrs. Chapman has decided to take early retirement," Dean Williams said, "and with that, there is a full-time position open. The board has decided to offer you the position."

Emily's eyes lit up with delight when she heard the news and that she had won the silent game she thought she was having with Williams.

"Then I take it that you are interested?" he asked.

Emily didn't realize she hadn't said anything and that the look of excitement would be enough.

Before she opened her mouth, Dean Williams continued, "Before you answer for sure, you need to be aware of a couple of things."

Concerned, Emily squinted her eyes like she had an idea what Williams was going to say. While Marie-Glen was an exceptional school, it was not without its challenges when educating children. There was a class of children that the school administration put together to increase their understanding of the curriculum. Emily never liked the term "slower learners," but that is what the class was. Maybe "kids who need more practice" was a better one? *No. Too long.*

"As you may or may not know, Mrs. Chapman was one of our best teachers. She took struggling students and helped get them to the next level of their education," Williams proclaimed before he continued. "But there have been students that she couldn't help in the way she thought she could for one reason or another."

Emily decided to have a voice in the conversation. "Dean Williams," she said, "Why did Mrs. Chapman retire this early in the school year?"

Williams sat back in his chair and replied with the flimsiest of excuses, "Well, she could have retired a year ago, but decided to stay on…and, but then she realized that she shouldn't have."

"Okay," Emily said, nodding her head, "Now I am going to ask the same question again, and I would appreciate it if you didn't blow smoke up my ass." *Oof. That probably wasn't necessary.*

Dean Williams smiled where most people in supervisory positions would frown. Even though their personalities clashed, there was still an air of respect he had towards her.

"Why did Mrs. Chapman retire this early in the year?"

Dean Williams leaned in, appreciating her tenacity. "Ms. Sinclair," he said earnestly, "This class may be the most challenging to teach that this school has ever seen. You will need to teach a child that doesn't speak English to read and write along with the other students. You will have students from other city schools because they decided to move the areas to what schools. Some come from the inner city, others from a more rural area. Perhaps the biggest challenge is to communicate with a deaf child and learn just as well as the rest." There was something wrong with that last sentence, not from the task's hardship, but the vernacular.

"Why not just put the deaf child in a special school?" Emily asked.

"Too far and too expensive," Williams replied. There was another round of silence as the second-hand kept clacking ominously.

Now was the time to ask questions. Emily had the opportunity in front of her, but she decided not to voice her concerns like she always did. Coming off as scared or unsure of herself could lessen her likelihood of becoming full-time. After waiting for so long, Emily did not want to risk her potential career.

"Was there another question?" Dean Williams asked.

Yes, but Emily didn't want him to know that. "I don't think so," Emily answered.

Williams raised his eyebrow, and he smirked at Emily's tenaciousness. "This isn't the time to be reserved," he stated, "This is not a normal situation for many teachers. In fact, some need special training for this kind of, um, circumstance."

Emily knew from that last comment that Dean Williams had a problem with trying to be politically correct. "Are you suggesting that these kids are going to be a problem for me?" Emily asked.

"Not at all," he answered, defending himself, "In fact, I think you may be the most qualified."

Emily wanted to smile but didn't want to make it evident that she was excited.

"If you really think I am suited, then I will take the job," she said. Emily hid her excitement underneath a veil of professionalism. It was the least she could do to make Dean forget about them butting heads earlier.

"I do think so," Williams rebutted.

"Great," Emily quickly said.

"Then, you want it?"

"I do."

"Good," he replied with a raised voice.

"Excellent," she calmly said.

It was like watching a father and daughter trying to get the last word before the girl stomped up the stairs and into her room before slamming the door. Both were not sure why they were getting so intense with each other at the time.

"Great," Williams said with a sigh.

Emily nodded, and they sat in silence as the clock ticked away the seconds.

"Well," he began, leaning forward in his chair and smiling, "let's meet your new class." Emily started to shudder as they stood up to leave his office. *New class.* Those were the words that scared her the most. There was always something about the word new that rattled the fiber of one's being to the bone. The truth is that no one really wants the "new" at first sometimes. Dramatically changing your life is terrifying, but then to be put in charge of someone else's children for a year is something else altogether.

3

Why do all elementary schools that have been open for decades always have that smell? Emily asked herself as she walked down the first-floor hallway to her new classroom. Emily was convinced that it was some amalgamation of Pine-Sol, bleach, and kid puke. It never failed. They all have that scent until you get used to it and just call it "work." *This must be how cat owners are so oblivious that their house smells like cat piss; they just get used to it.*"

The walk to Room 114, located in the third-grade end of the school, seemed more like a slow shuffle to the electric chair than the victory that Emily had built up in her mind. She wasn't sure what she agreed to other than a full-time job. The idea of having to communicate with other kids who were not deemed adept as the rest of the school had not sunk in yet. She looked down at the recently polished floors that led to the end of the hall and began to panic. As the dean led the way, Emily attempted to keep her mind off the possible future. She could ultimately fail at such an attempt by looking at the pea green lockers that hadn't seen a fresh coat of paint since the late '90s. Even with that, they just used the same paint leftovers from the 70's so they could keep the school expenses down. The lockers bothered Emily as she believed that the school's look always resembled a prison more than it did a school.

Mr. Williams and Emily Sinclair both stood in front of Room 114, waiting for the worst. "Are you ready?" Williams asked.

Emily took a deep breath and hesitated to respond.

Dean Williams took note of Emily's reluctance, and he asked for the first, last, and only time, "Are you sure you are ready for this? You can have the rest of the day to think about it."

Emily put her tongue behind her front teeth as; It was a way to help her concentrate or a sign that she was getting irritated. At that moment, reality had settled in. *If I don't do it, who will? There is no guarantee that they would do any better.* Education is just like any other job globally; some come and do the best they can with what they have. Hopefully, they make an impact on a child, if only for a moment. Then some come for the paycheck and do nothing. Emily always knew that she wanted to make an impact in life one way or another. Hopefully, this is how she did it.

"I can do this," she told him. Dean Williams put his hand on the doorknob, and as he opened the door to the sound of children talking loudly, he replied, "I hope you're right."

It wasn't that it was overbearingly noisy in the classroom. It was more that it was hard to understand what was going on. Usually, there was a sense of understanding and comradery in a class that went hand in hand. Emily knew that it would be ignorant to think that every child would get along, but she felt that there would be an ounce of friendship established somehow; there wasn't any. Loud voices argued over petty things. Different dialects and accents came from every direction where God probably didn't even know what was happening in the classroom.

Dean Williams sighed at the sight of youth at its worst. He leaned into Emily's ear and whispered, "Good luck to you, and I sincerely mean that." For the first time in her early teaching career, Emily Sinclair feared children, which isn't an ideal situation when you must teach them.

4

After hearing the story of her first official day as a full-time teacher, Paul was fascinated by the rest of the stories that Emily could tell. "You had quite the uphill battle," he stated.

Emily, feeling very defeated after only a few minutes of talking to a therapist, was in no mood for juvenile tones. She scoffed and asked, "If we're going to have some kind of banter between us, could you please refrain from talking to me like a child?"

He didn't. Emily's anxiety had taken over, and she became agitated.

Paul fidgeted in his chair, not knowing what to say. In his experience, most people respond better to simple questions when they have difficult times.

Emily started to hear noises. She tilted her head around, trying to make heads of where the noise was coming from. That didn't stop her from lying to the man trying to help. "It was an uphill battle," she exclaimed, "I told you that in the story. That was the point I was making. I don't need you dumbing down what I already have said! If we're going to play that game, I will go ahead and give you short answers! Thank you for repeating what I just said differently. You must have been at the top of your class with skills like that! Do me a favor and talk to me like you're a normal fucking human being! And what the hell is that noise?"

Emily jumped out from her seat and started to crawl on the tile floors. Germs didn't matter to Emily anyway, but with clean floors like Dr. Cusick had, there was no need to be concerned. *Skitch, skitch, skitch.* It was like fingernails against a faraway chalkboard. Emily scooted her way to the middle of the room, running into an end table that almost resulted in a broken lamp.

"What is it that you're doing?" Paul asked after her tantrum.

Emily took her ear away from the floor, and she gave him a concerned look. "You mean you don't hear that?" She put her right ear back to the floor. *Click-click-tat-tat-tat-tat.* It was them. Emily just knew it was the faint chatter of their teeth.

Bam. The floor vibrated, startling Emily as it rattled the area she currently occupied. She looked back at her therapist and stared at him, waiting for him to acknowledge the sound. "Sorry," she said, "I thought I saw a bug." The noises had stopped, and Emily laid her head back on the floor in defeat.

"What is it you heard?" Paul asked.

Emily slightly shook her head in disbelief that he would believe her. "The kids," she answered, "They follow me. They have for a while now, close to a month, and they just get closer and closer. The noises they make with their mouths are unnerving, and it makes me want to lock myself in a steel box and swallow the key."

Paul stood from his seat and walked over to Emily on the floor. As he took his first step, the room became a tad brighter, like a light bulb receiving too many electrical energy watts.

He sat down next to Emily and stated, "That's okay, but I am going to sit Indian style right here and talk to you until you decide to get up. Is that okay?"

"Crisscross applesauce," Emily mumbled.

"Pardon?" Paul pondered.

"You can't say Indian style anymore when describing that sitting position. It's culturally insensitive, so you say crisscross applesauce instead," Emily answered without an ounce of inflection in her voice. She looked at Paul, waiting for a response, only to find a hint of confusion on his face.

Emily laid back down and continued, "I know. It's retarded."

Paul grinned and stated, "Now I am pretty sure you're not supposed to say that anymore."

Emily rolled over onto her back and looked at the white ceiling with no flaws. "It doesn't really matter at this point," she said with melancholy in her voice, "No one pays me any attention anymore. They see me on the streets or in the store, and they look the other way. Well, most of them do."

"We'll get back to that in a bit, but since you want me to cut all the B.S., I need to ask a question that is to the point."

"Thank God," Emily roared, "What is it?"

"Why do you think these children are following you? They could go anywhere else. Why stick with you? Did you teach these kids? Were they in your class?"

Emily sat up and angled her legs so she could lay her head on her knees. "I was a substitute teacher before, so I probably did at some point."

"Why you, though?" Paul asked, "There were others involved in the incident after all."

Emily, tired of being upset and sounding defeated, replied, "If I knew that, I wouldn't be here."

"Maybe it was something I did. Maybe it's something I didn't do." She answered honestly, "But maybe there is just no justification in death. That's the answer I am leaning toward."

Skitch. Skitch. Skitch.

"There they are, again.," Emily said, defeated.

Any person who was curious enough would have climbed onto the floor to listen for what Emily had heard, but not Paul. He was a professional, and joining her would add to her possible and troubling psychosis.

"It's strange," Emily said, "the ones that follow me…, the ones with the crystal blue pupils with eyelids that look like they are painted white don't know. But the kids, my kids, the ones in class, look normal to me except for the black eyes and smog around them. The black eyes that look like someone sprayed graffiti on them, and the paint dripped down their cheeks."

Emily sat up and looked at her new therapist to ask the simple question, "Why would the dead look so different?"

Paul could have easily thrown around some cultural beliefs that he had heard or read about overtime stemming from Asia. Europe's dark eyes typically go the more traditional route with the supernatural, but that was not what Emily wanted to hear. "Maybe I could get a better idea and make a hypothesis if I knew more about some of your students."

The Fair and Inclusive
System of Kids

Emily was never one to suffer from any kind of stage fright. She had no problem expressing herself in any form manner she deemed appropriate. Only people seemed to focus on when Emily shot her mouth off to defend what she believed to be accurate. *Funny how people who do not like to be contested outside of social media are always valid.* This day was different, though. She was not facing other adults as she was used to as she would have had a stiff drink and stimulating conversation with them. Today was when she needed to shut her mouth and forget her personal beliefs several hours a day. She was about to engage young, impressionable children regularly now.

She stood behind her desk, trying to find the right angle to lay her purse down while staring at the number of kids in her new classroom; fifteen to be exact. She was now responsible for teaching fifteen of the most supposedly unteachable kids in Marie-Glen Elementary. Under most circumstances, the teacher is the first to introduce themselves to a class. Still, a girl named Sloane Chastain started the conversation.

"You're very pretty," Sloane said.

Taken aback by the compliment, Emily thanked her. "My name is Ms. Sincl—" Emily began before the conversation amongst the class continued.

"Do you have a boyfriend?" a boy from the back asked as he raised his hand, which defeated the purpose.

"Well…," Emily tried to begin again.

"Of course, she does, pea-brain. Look at her!" Sloane replied with a hint of arrogance in her voice.

Sloane Chastain was the type of girl usually described as "that one girl in every school." The stuck-up one that didn't acknowledge other kids unless they fell into some type of mold or that she just wanted to insult them instead. Sloane's parents were the type that only kept the company of like-minded people. They weren't necessarily rich or needed material things that many would assume based on Sloan's personality. They just wanted to have a discussion and opinions with which others agreed. *You know...like the internet.* Sloane clung to this in a way that alienated her from other children growing up. If you asked the kids in her school what they thought of Sloane, they'd say, *"You'd think I crapped my pants because when I try to talk to her, her nose in the air,"* or *"I heard that she has a fit if she doesn't get Starbucks in the morning.".* These were all actual quotes that Emily had heard over time.

"Is it serious?" the boy in the back asked, continuing his inquiry about her relationship status.

Emily was not going to get a word in during this conversation. She was curious about how the discussion regarding her love life was going to end without any input. It was like her parents' dinner parties all over again. Judging by her appearance, Sloane was a well-behaved and well-dressed child. The reality was that she had dyslexia—double deficit dyslexia, to be exact.

Sloane Chastain had difficulty isolating sounds when reading. She had a problem with naming letters and numbers when she saw them. There were other children in Marie-Glen elementary with dyslexia. Still, Sloane's was nothing the district had ever seen before; hence she was in that classroom. "Yeah. Like you have a shot," Sloane sneered, implying Brad was not good enough as she tried to get a laugh from others. She looked around the classroom to find a smile or a snicker, but her rep made it where no one wanted to acknowledge her.

"I bet there is someone better," the boy continued, raising his eyebrows up and down, indicating he was the someone. Brad Medler was the class mouthpiece. If there was a joke or a jab at someone, Brad was usually the culprit. "My brother says that most girls don't know what a real man is like," Brad continued as he winked at Emily.

Emily winced. She couldn't believe the way kids talked compared to when she grew up.

A deep voice came from the right side of the class as Derek Singletary replied, "I'm sure she'll let you know when she finds one."

The class erupted in an instigative *"Ooooh" and "Buurrrnnn!"* It wasn't unusual for Derek and Brad to butt heads, and in this instance, Brad rose from his seat with his arms out, indicating he wanted to start a fight. Derek, who had been looking for a reason to throw down, rose as well. Derek was one of three African American children at Marie-Glen. Unfortunately, they were in regular classes, which made it hard for him to communicate with others. He wasn't comfortable in his skin because it was not like the rest of his classmates. It is sad when people can't just be satisfied with one another that looks different. Human psychology is at its purest and worst.

Here we go. Emily had to speak up and take control of the classroom finally. "Ok, sit down and let me speak before you embarrass yourselves," Emily intervened.

Both the boys stared each other down before they sat back down in their seats.

"As I was saying, my name is Ms. Sinclair, and I will be your new teacher for the rest of the year." A small arm from the left of the room was raised for the first time without someone already talking. Emily pointed to a chubby, rose-cheeked boy named Bo Gentry to allow him to speak.

"Why'd the other teacher leave fer?" His accent was thick. It was evident that Bo was not from the Midwest as Emily detected a Southern inflection. *Oh, thank God I am not the only hillbilly here.*

"Mrs. Chapman decided to take her retirement early…kind of," Emily answered. The class looked around at one another, and while some laughed, others looked disappointed.

"You mean she gave up," a meek voice said from the front row. A small brown-haired girl with thick-lensed glasses looked up at Emily with a crooked smile. The class seemed surprised that she spoke, but Emily wasn't sure why.

"What's your name, sweetie?" Emily asked. The girl leaned back with her head down again; clothes were coming apart. Small holes appeared in her blue button-up shirt from the silverfish that occupied her home. "Ava Nauling," the girl answered. It was apparent to Emily that Ava was timid and that it would be tough to get her to talk, but this was a start.

"You have a beautiful name, Ava," Emily told her, "Sometimes people work for so long that they can retire and be with their families more. That's all."

Ava nodded her head and leaned back over her desk with a pencil in her hand, ready to work. Emily knew that she wasn't buying it. It wasn't a lie necessarily, but Mrs. Chapman retired earlier than planned because it became too hard to handle. Emily was confident that it was just due to not understanding kids nowadays. Still, that idea would quickly dissipate over time.

"I am going to go ahead and take roll call," Emily proclaimed to the class. As she went down the list, she came upon the name Jamie Renee Cassidy. As she spoke her name, there was no response. Emily looked around the class and noticed a girl with short dirty blonde hair peeping out of the window, not paying attention, repeating her name with no response.

Emily grew agitated. She was not used to being ignored; she wasn't being missed, but rather, unheard.

A girl named Tonya raised her hand. She informed Emily, "That's Jamie Renee." She pointed her out, and it was the same girl that Emily suspected.

Before she could raise her voice, another child clarified what Emily had already learned: "She's deaf, so it's hard to get her attention."

Emily's body deflated slightly from releasing the air she would use to yell across the room that wouldn't have done any good. She gazed across the room and saw an Asian boy, Feng Song, sitting in isolation and quiet. It occurred to Emily that she would have a communication issue from two different directions: the inability to hear and not knowing the English language. *I am not sure if I can do this.*

Emily took the first day of her new position to assess her class. Two students on opposite sides of the room, Feng Song and Jamie Renee didn't speak or attempt communication, nor did they appear to be interested. It would take a while for Emily to understand what she was contending with for each student finally. Their different problems in life would prove difficult to bring them together as a whole. In front of the wooden podium, Emily stood in front of the school provided for each classroom that looked like it existed when Lincoln gave the Gettysburg Address. Each nick in the wood had a piece of history attached to it in some way. While Marie-Glen needed a huge update, the nostalgia was enough to keep Emily happy.

2

Paul listened intently to Emily's recollection of her first official day of class. Hearing her talk about it so vividly gave him hope that she could come back from the horrors in her mind for a while longer. "So, how did you feel about that day when you got home?" Paul asked.

Emily squinted her eyes and started to think awfully hard about later that night. She could remember the day, but not her time at home with Crosby, her fiancé, afterward. "I don't remember much. I remember being very tired and talking about my day to Crosby. He listened to all of my hopes and fears as we laid in bed that night," she explained. Emily found her way back onto the couch by then and put her feet under her, leaning on the left arm.

"What was he like?" Paul asked.

Emily shrugged her shoulders and replied, "He was my college crush."

Paul smiled and laughed a bit. "Is that all?" he asked.

Emily smiled and breathed in heavily like the start of a yawn. "Of course not," she said, "He was the guy in the middle."

Paul, with a confused grimace on his face, asked, "The middle?"

"Crosby was the guy in the middle; at least that's what I referred to it. He was one of the guys that everyone knew and liked well enough, but he never really belonged to any cliques. Crosby wasn't that athletic, wasn't a genius, at least that we knew of. He was just Crosby Fulton, the class nerd that happened to be into the pop culture things that kids love now so much now. Back when we were in elementary school, if anyone knew that he read comics or liked sci-fi, he would have been teased. He is all those things, but what many people don't see about him is how funny and sweet he actually is."

Paul leaned in and assumed a "but" was coming up, but there wasn't. "You make him sound like he was the perfect man," Paul said.

Emily shook her head but then digressed with, "I mean, he may have been for me, but he wasn't perfect."

Paul noticed that Emily used the past tense just then, so he had to inquire about it. "What do you mean '"may have been"?'"

Emily's glee she was having with the conversation took a turn for the melancholy suddenly. "Things happened, and words were said that I, we, can't take back now," she explained.

"Why can't you—"

Paul began to inquire before Emily interjected with a raised voice, "It doesn't matter!"

A long pause between Emily and Paul, the man that presumably got paid to ask questions, made the session awkward for a few moments. After the tense moment had passed, Emily laid her hand on her face to lean on. With her eyes closed, she asked, "Have you ever known love where no matter how much older you get, the other person still sees you as you were when you first met? How would you go to bed, make love, and spend the entire night talking until you realized that it was morning? I miss that. I would give anything for that to be true again."

"Why can't it?" Paul inquired. He knew the truth already, but he had to make sure Emily said it.

"He left. He left, and I was too proud to stop him. I really needed him after what happened, but he wasn't there…not for me." Emily began to think about her apartment and how lonely it was. There was a smell that Crosby had that she loved, and it could be detected as soon as you walked through the front door. Emily didn't know it then, but she needed that smell as it subconsciously made her feel less stressed and anxious. The vision of coming home to a man waiting for you to arrive through the door was a pure pleasure that Emily took for granted. She didn't realize what it meant until it was gone. *I suppose that is true for most people.*

As Emily pushed back her pain and tears, Paul asked, "What happened when you finally came home after the tragedy?"

3

Emily came home early the next morning in the clothes she wore to class the day before. It was all a blur afterward. She thought she had come back from the hospital after being examined for injuries and other trauma signs. Everything that happened the day before was becoming all mixed together in her mind, and all she wanted to do was try to go to sleep as best she could. She reached inside her purse only to find that it wasn't on her shoulder. *Shit,* she thought, *I must have left it in the hospital.* She noticed that the door to her apartment was cracked open. Nervously pushing on the door, she expected someone to be inside. Possibly someone that wanted to hurt her; perhaps it was a disgruntled parent. *It wasn't my fault.*

When Emily and Crosby started looking for apartments in, or around, Marie-Glen, they knew they didn't want a typical residence. Finding a house would probably prove impossible as many of the homes ranged from half a million dollars into the millions; that and they weren't ready for that kind of commitment yet. Instead, they decided to try renting a house, and when that didn't work, they investigated other options. The easy way would have been to find a nearby place within the Cincinnati area, but they didn't want to do that because they liked Marie-Glen too much. They and were obsessed with the idea of it and what the future could hold for them there. So, they did what ordinary people in their mid to late twenties did in the new century; they took more of a hipster route.

The home would eventually be a small apartment above an antique store that an older woman named Claire Dubois owned. The building was as old as the town itself, so the pipes were loud, and the floorboards creaked. Ms. Dubois didn't seem to mind too much as she was hard of hearing anyway. Not only did she occupy the downstairs for business, but she also used it as a small apartment. Emily and Crosby couldn't have been luckier to find their abode, and they knew it. The living room window was crescent-shaped and divided into four equal parts separated by oak. When they looked out of it, they could view the small downtown area where other shops were visible. There was a roundabout in the town center that kept traffic flowing smoothly, and people rode bikes without a care in the world. That was the dream, to live somewhere with little to no worry. Emily and Crosby didn't have to do anything; they could just look out the window and watch everything going on from above.

Emily walked into her apartment for the first time in what seemed like a week; it was cold and felt empty. Deep down, Emily hoped that Crosby would be there. *Maybe the news of what happened would bring him back,* she thought. As she walked into the living room, Emily saw a sheet of folded paper on the coffee table next to the tan sectional sofa they bought together. Their first piece of furniture was, in fact. *Jesus, that sofa was a pain to get up here.*

It just laid y there begging to be touched, to be opened, and with all her will, she simply leaned over it to view the inside of it. Emily convinced herself that it was a goodbye letter from Crosby. Their argument from the night before undoubtedly prompted him to pack up his bags and leave.

Tilting her head uncomfortably, Emily looked at the font to see that it was merely a flyer for the upcoming autumn festival in town.

Emily sighed and walked into the kitchen to brew some coffee, which was probably the last thing she needed as she hadn't stopped shaking since the day before. The shaking wasn't of concern, but the need for sleep was. She was so tired, but her visions started to come to her mind every time she shut her eyes: gunfire, blood splatter, and her running toward her students.

The air in the apartment was still. There wasn't the clanking of an old pipe when Emily turned on the faucet or the creaking of the longstanding floorboards. The life that Emily and Crosby put into their home, that small apartment, was gone. As much emptiness as Emily felt, it didn't compare to the desolation of the world around her. Crosby didn't say goodbye to her. Not a phone call, not a letter, not a wave goodbye, not a passive-aggressive "fuck you," nothing. Out of all the times to leave her, this day was the worst time to do it as she needed Crosby more than ever. Still, he was gone, and as far as Emily was concerned, everything terrible happening in her life was her fault.

Narcissist. Don't make this all about you right now! There was more going on right now with everyone in town that was bigger than her. An act of evil had shaken this community to its core, and Emily needed to be there as best she could even though she didn't want to be. The thought of facing everyone—the reporters, the parents of the children—was just unbearable. She just couldn't. Not yet, anyway.

Emily looked out of her living room window at a town whose streets were covered in news vans and reporters running around aimlessly, attempting to obtain quotes from the locals. As she looked downward, she saw people standing outside of her building. With looks of despair draped in sadness on their faces, parents started pointing at the facility and eventually up toward Emily's apartment. Emily gasped and stepped back because she didn't want anyone to see her, but it was too late. The sounds of moans from outside began to haunt Emily. She slowly walked back toward the window, and as she became visible, the children on the street started to point. Awful, haunting wails came from their tiny mouths that grew unnaturally bigger the longer they cried. Thin, black sludge began to drip from their teeth onto their chins.

Their skin was white with gray hints that highlighted the tiny, shrunken faces, and black smoke surrounded their frail bodies. The children were her students shrouded in darkness and seemingly cursed by her presence. It would never occur to Emily that the children were her curse because she survived. She had to think of herself as the bad guy because there was no other excuse in her post-traumatic reasoning. She let it happen, which Emily deserved even though she would say otherwise out loud to the ghosts that haunted her. Guilt is an endless shadow that we cast upon ourselves.

Their eyes were gone, leaving only dark pits with oozing thick, black liquid that leaked down their pale faces as they cried and moaned louder. *Why can't they talk? Why are they making that noise!? What are you trying to say?* The children, with their small, dead hearts, couldn't speak. The blackness that invaded their eyes also oozed out of their mouth and fell onto the ground beneath them.

Emily put her hand over her mouth and began to cry. The parents looked up at her, and they silently judged her. *How could you? Look at what you did!* That's what Emily thought they were saying to themselves. She didn't, no, she couldn't understand. "Can't you see them next to you?" she yelled out loud. Emily recognized some parents from parent/teacher conferences, especially the big man and woman in the front of the crowd. She looked down and saw Bo Gentry's parents looking up at her apartment. They had a look of defeat in their eyes; it was the look a person has when nothing else matters anymore. You exist in this world without anything to cling to.

Stepping back from the window, Emily collapsed on the couch nearby and cried herself to sleep. *It wasn't my fault. I did the best I could.* Those were the thoughts Emily had that night and for many nights after that, but it was this day when she became convinced that she had started to go mad. After a while, she would wake up, but nothing seemed real anymore. It was like everything was a dream, and Emily was floating through life, but it would quickly become wrapped in what nightmares were made of when Emily left her home. Emily wasn't sure what was worse; that she was still alive or that they were all dead.

4

Emily snuck her hand in her purse after a long pause in the conversation with Paul. Going through the contents of her bag with only her hand and the memory of what she had previously, she couldn't find just one damn cigarette. Paul had seen this desperate move before with other people. He found it humorous that they thought they were sneaky by trying to smoke indoors, but it wasn't exactly very cloak and dagger.

"There is no smoking, Ms. Sinclair," he said sternly.

Emily gently pulled her hand out of her purse and replied, "Emily, please. When you are proper, it makes me think my mother is here."

While not exactly a question for this type of dilemma, Paul asked, "Do you not like your mother?"

Emily laughed to herself and answered, "I suppose so. I mean, we don't have much in common, but we don't argue. In fact, we don't do much at all."

"Does that bother you?" Paul inquired.

Emily put her finger in the air and waved it at Paul. "No," she inferred, "You are not going to do that shrink thing and put everything on my mother, or father for that matter."

"Sometimes, when we see the faults in people we were close to. We sometimes see it in ourselves when talking about it out loud," Paul pointed out, trying to give some insight to his query.

"Are you trying to say that I am just like my mother? That's every woman's music to her ears. I bet dating you would be just a hoot," Emily nervously joked. She tried to get rid of the shaking throughout her body that she had started to feel suddenly.

Paul found Emily's quick wit humbling but was more concerned with her potential mental breakdown. "Are you okay?" he asked simply.

Emily put the fingers she used to hold a cigarette up to her mouth, took a fake drag, and blew out imaginary smoke. *They say that mimicking the act of smoking can help.*

"My, my, doc. That is a loaded question, but if I were, I wouldn't be here, now would I?" Paul smiled, nodded, and replied, "Of course. I just meant at this current moment."

No, moron. "I'm fine," Emily lied, "I guess I am waiting to find out if I am certifiable yet."

Paul shifted in his seat and sighed, "I haven't quite heard enough yet to come to that point, but don't worry. If you see a couple of burly men come in with a stretcher and a funny-looking jacket with long arms, then you will know."

Paul was kidding, but Emily was not in the mood. "Paul. Mr. Cusick. I need you to do me a really big fuckin' solid right now and not blow smoke up my ass. I need to know if paying your fee is going to screw me in the end."

Paul hadn't heard many patients curse like that in such a short amount of time before. Not to his knowledge, at least. He knew heading into the session that Emily could be a bit of a hothead. "Just trying to lighten the mood, I suppose," Paul playfully defended, "but your fee is being handled by an outside source."

"Who?"

Paul debated telling Emily his answer, but the one he knew he was going to go with was, "The school board is covering this session."

In a sardonic tone, Emily, surprised by the notion, said, "That's surprising, to say the least."

"Why is that?"

Another damn question. "I'm sure you have it in your file somewhere. The many times I got into trouble with the board, or from the parents in general." It wasn't a secret that Emily moved to the beat of her own drum with teaching and disciplinary tactics. "I was just trying to make a point and tell the kids and parents what they needed to hear. I was just trying to make them better than the system gave them credit for."

Paul took a drink of water from a nearby mug and asked, "How? I am curious how you taught these supposed lost causes."

Emily shrugged her shoulders and replied, "You can't rely on a lesson plan, a piece of chalk, and a blackboard." Emily paused to give a quick complaint. "A blackboard. A blackboard? That school was so stuck in the past and up its own ass. They refused to get with the times. Get a whiteboard with markers, for God's sake."

The Empathy Project

Paul knew a lot about Emily before setting foot through his office's doors, most of which came from the higher-ups. He didn't know and pondered about most throughout the session how one person could manage a group of children with such different developmental issues. He remembered reading a paper about a psychiatrist in Indiana who conducted group sessions where everyone had an unusual mental affliction. The psychiatric program wasn't completed due to the hospital's destruction from a natural disaster. *That meteor really did a number on that place.*

This situation was not any different in many ways. Still, people like Paul and others, even more, qualified to take on case studies, are trained to think about social issues; Emily was not. There was no guidebook given to teachers about these rare situations, and there was only one way to find out.

"So, how did you manage to do this for a year?" Paul inquired.

Emily tilted her head as she didn't understand the question. "What do you mean exactly?"

"The children. They were special cases in this town according to what you were telling me, so I am wondering how you made it work," Paul clarified.

Emily scoffed at the question in disgust.

"Did I offend you somehow?" Paul asked with a calm demeanor.

It wasn't his fault. Anyone who hadn't worked within the public school system probably never would. "No," Emily replied empathetically, "You didn't. It was actually for two years."

Paul fumbled through his notes, not knowing that Emily spent her two school years with the same class. "If you want to get technical, it was more like a year and a half, if even that." Paul started to flick the pen against his two front teeth, frustrated with not knowing this information.

"Two years," Paul stated, flabbergasted at the thought.

Emily nodded her head, "Yep. They wanted me to stay with them because they saw some progress and didn't want to make drastic changes to these kids' lives. At least that is what they told me." *It was a flimsy excuse.*

Emily had nothing to lose at this point in her life, especially when she could be completely certifiable. The issues with her work building up for months had finally come to a head when Paul asked how she solved her students' problems.

"You want to know the flat-out truth about my students, Paul?" she asked, "There is nothing wrong with them. They can learn like anyone else, but no one takes the time to do it. If someone doesn't read fast enough, then they are given a label. Another is deaf, and she becomes hard to teach. It's not easy to teach people, but sometimes educators just need to rearrange their thought processes. No one is willing to do that, and even if there are good teachers that are willing to do it, the schools don't shell out the funding to pay them to do so. Then what happens? They are thrown in a room, isolated from others that can help them. All these kids want—all anyone wants---is to be included. They weren't, and that can make anyone feel bad, stupid, or alone, even from their own families that should support them the most. All I did was try to make them feel included and better about the school. All I got was reprimanded for it because it is not how they did things at that school, even when what they were doing wasn't working."

"So, what did you do, exactly? I mean, what was the moment that you really sprang into action, so to speak."

Emily looked up in the air pondering how to answer Paul's question. *Do I do this eloquently, or do I just make it short and sweet as possible? Screw it.*

"The same way most people start doing things that are important, someone pissed me off."

2

The class clown, Brad Medler, knew how to press all the wrong buttons, especially Emily's. Brad was not a class clown in the traditional sense. Like putting their hands underneath their armpits to make flatulent noises or making goofy faces behind someone else's back. To be fair, it was all those things as well, but Brad went to a crueler route at his classmate's expense.

Emily did her best to try to teach the curriculum as best she could. She was translating the details as best she could to the class, especially Jamie and Feng. The hardest part was making sure that they genuinely understood the assignments and how to proceed with them. Feng was the biggest challenge with the language barrier. *At least Jamie could read the assignment notes.*

Sometimes Emily just sat in her chair and watched the kids talk to one another, and what she found was that they weren't really. Everyone seemed to be isolated from one another in some way, ranging from pure shyness to not knowing the English language; it was strange. She remembered a time in elementary school where the teacher had to be on the ball to make sure the kids were doing their work, but not with this lot. It was more about making sure they knew how to do the job.

"Okay, everyone," Emily announced as she waved her hand in the air to make sure everyone would know that time was up on the math quiz they had. "Go ahead and pass the papers to the right, and we will go over our work." The sound of paper flapping in the air was like music to her ears. It was the sound of not having to grade any papers that night. Everyone passed to the right except Ava, who looked confused as she looked to the wrong side.

"Your other right, Ava," Emily instructed her with a smile. Ava smirked and gave her paper to her neighbor.

"Wait," Paul interrupted, "What happens to the people sitting to the right side of the room?"

Emily rolled her eyes and sighed, "What?"

"The papers of the kids sitting on the right. If your class has lined up desks, then where do those papers go?"

Emily struggled to understand what Paul was asking.

"Who grades the papers of the kids sitting on the right side of the class?" he asked, slowing down the sentence's pace.

"Oh!" Emily exclaimed, "They get up and bring it to the kids on the left side."

Paul nodded and let Emily continue with the story.

Starting with the first problem of about twenty, the kids read the answer aloud, and if it was not correct, they had to state what they thought the right answer was. It eventually became Feng Song's turn in the class, the time in school that Feng hated the most; reading the explanation, heck, any translation of the English language in general.

"Okay, Feng," Emily said as she went to the board to write, "the problem is twenty-four divided by six. What is the answer they gave on the paper?"

Nervously, Feng stood and answered with, "Fo."

Emily knew exactly what he meant, even with Feng's thick accent. *He could enunciate more, but we'll work on it.* "Okay, was that correct?" Emily asked the class.

Feng was confused by the question. Emily figured it might have been that he did not know the word "correct." "Is four correct?" she rephrased.

"Oh!" he said, "Hai…I mean, yes."

Nodding her head in agreement, Emily asked the entire class if that was the correct answer. They unanimously agreed, except that Brad had a slightly different response: "Fo sho!"

The class giggled a bit, and as they laughed to themselves, Emily watched Feng's face go from a moment of proudness to that of shame. "Brad!" she yelled across the room.

"Hai…I mean yes," he mockingly repeated at Feng's expense.

"That is the last time," she told Brad.

Brad scoffed and gave a sarcastic "Okay."

After a few more questions and answers from the children, Jamie Renee's turn came to be. She stood up to answer the question as Emily wrote down the problem for the entire class, mostly Feng and Jamie. It was awkward for Emily to talk to Jamie as she still wondered if she could read lips. Pointing to the board's problem, Jamie was asked, "What is twenty-seven divided by nine?" She looked around the classroom as she struggled to find the word within what voice she could muster without hearing it.

"Thwee," Jaime said. Just like Feng before her, after she got the thumbs up from her teacher, Emily Sinclair, Jamie felt like she could do anything. Everyone in this world deserves a moment to be proud of what they accomplish. Unfortunately, it only takes one bad apple to bring down that temporary high. That sour, rotting apple that was a scourge over the entire room was Brad Medler.

"Thwee!" Brad mockingly proclaimed to the class, "Ar ooh soor?" It was demeaning enough for someone to make fun of how a person talks because of their shortcomings, but Brad Medler took it to another level. Brad brought his right hand up to his chest. He then tilted the side of it and lightly beat it against his chest, implying that Jamie had a mental disability, which she did not.

Brad then started to imitate a person in a wheelchair that needed a voice interpreter. In a mock robot voice, he said, "If a deaf person swears, does their mother wash their hands with soap?"

Jamie looked around the room and watched as the classroom laughed at Brad's tasteless jokes. Most children laughed not because Brad made a joke at Jaime's expense but because Brad was making funny faces and talking funny. Jamie's bottom lip began to quiver, and suddenly she dashed away from her seat to the front door crying.

Emily didn't stop her, not because she didn't care, but she was busy thinking about the next course of action.

Emily had always heard the saying, "I saw red," when someone described getting angry but never understood it until that day. Her vision temporarily became askew, and she could feel her blood pressure rise. At the time, Emily could have sworn that she saw red, maybe a blood vessel in her eye burst. Perhaps it was just in her mind as she wanted to be a bull in Spain after the cocky matador with the red muleta. Brad Medler was the proverbial muleta, and Emily was the bull that tried to take him down.

Emily, for the first time in her life, thought about tearing off another person's head. She never thought of herself as a violent person. Emily. She was usually guilty of shooting her mouth off due to her southern temperament, sure, but never physical violence. That changed as she watched Brad Medler laughing with his over-styled black hair and his oversized two front teeth exposed. *His teeth annoyed me. I am not sure why, but he looked like he could eat an apple through a chained fence.*

Brad never saw it coming; the rage that she never felt toward another person seethed. He was about to get an earful from someone that had never heard a human voice in her life. *Oh. You thought it was me? No! I would have been fired on the spot for violently touching another child.*

Jamie Renee stormed back into the classroom bringing back her hand, and slapped the ever-living Hell "*the ever-living hell*" out of Brad's face.

Like most bullies, Brad began to whimper as he fell out of his seat and flailed on the dirty floor. "Stop! Ow! Stop! Quit!" Brad cried, repeating those same words over again. Jamie's arms flailed about, hitting Brad Medler's body anywhere a fist could land. Emily Sinclair, Marie-Glen Elementary's professional teacher, slowly walked over to the fight because deep down, she thought that Brad was getting what he deserved. Emily wasn't proud of watching a student beat another in retrospect, but she enjoyed a proper comeuppance. *I never said I was a perfect teacher.*

Emily came back into reality and ran to Jamie to stop her from potentially breaking Brad's face. Trying to grab at the silk shirt Jamie was wearing, Emily kept trying to tell her to stop while forgetting that Jamie Renee was deaf. Jaime started shouting out what were probably curse words but were incoherent because of the screaming and pronunciation.

Jamie felt the palm of Emily's hand cover her head, pulling her towards her chest. Emily started to breathe as Jamie felt her chest move in and out, settling her down. The repetition of Emily's breathing and the sound of her heart began to pacify Jamie. The crying turned into runny nose sniffles. Emily knew there would be wet spots on her blue blouse from the tears and sweat, but it didn't bother her.

Brad slid up against the wall near his seat, wiping the blood from his nose. Young Medler didn't fare so well as his shirt had ripped, both sides of his nose bled, and his right eye swollen. A while back, Brad's older brother mentioned people with disabilities having what he referred to as "tard strength." That term went through his mind as he watched Jamie get cradled by Emily and not him. What he still didn't understand was that Jamie Renee was not a "tard,"; she was deaf and just got tired of Brad's desire to be humorous at her expense. Emily wasn't sure how long Brad had been torturing poor Jamie. It was enough time for her rage to come to a head that immediately rushed to her fists and eventually to his face.

Jamie pulled her head away from Emily's chest to find that she did indeed leave tear and snot marks that looked like part of a face on her blouse. Jamie put her hand into a fist and made a three-quarters circle on her chest as she whispered, "I'm sorry."

Emily took that piece of sign language to mind so she could try to communicate with Jamie better. Emily started to formulate a plan in her mind for the future, but that needed to be put on standby as there were other pressing matters.

As they both stood up, Jamie looked at Brad, who was still trying to compose himself from the beat down he had just endured. She put her right pointer finger to the end of her thumb, and she made a circle with her fingers sticking outward. Brad looked down at her hand, and as he brought his eyes up to see Jamie's face, she simply said, "Asshole!" *I'll have to remember that one as well.*

Emily sent Brad and Jamie to the principal's office, where their parents were called and brought in. Emily wasn't there for that meeting to see how the conversation went, but she wanted to be a fly on the wall during it. Based on Emily's information, Dean Williams decided to treat them like any other school student. He would have them serve a three-day suspension, which neither argued over. Emily was afraid of possible legal action from Emily's parents because of something her dad said when she got into a high school fight with a boy. While in math class, the boy started shooting rubber bands by hooking them to his braces, pulling back, and releasing them. To be fair, Emily asked him to "Stop, or I will break your face," but that didn't help as he did it again. Emily stormed out of her seat and began to punch his face repeatedly. After all that, her father never asked how she was. Instead, he posed the question, "What if their parents press charges?" That had always stuck with Emily over the years. Fortunately, neither set of parents' families talked about suing one another or even had anything hateful to say. They probably both knew they were in the wrong; however, both kids despised one another for a while—one for being a jerk and the other for physically beating them.

3

"She was the first one I saw, you know," Emily said to Paul after finishing part of her story.

Paul was confused about whether she was describing her past or if they were in a new conversation.

Emily saw Paul's confused expression and clarified, "Alone, I mean. I saw them together outside the apartment, but Jamie was the first one I saw individually."

Paul then decided to flip the page of his notebook to a fresh piece of paper.

Emily became interested in what Paul was writing. She raised her head a bit, trying to see any writing she could.

"Have I really talked enough to fill up a whole page?" she asked.

Paul shifted in his seat and replied, "Nothing for you to be concerned with."

Emily found that answer to be a bit curt and rude, but she let it go as he was there to help. Paul then continued by asking, "So why do you think she was the first one and not the rest?"

Emily rolled her eyes and sighed, "I don't know. I certainly didn't pick them out of a lineup and ask them to scare the shit out of me!"

Paul raised his hand to quell her temper quickly. "I'm not suggesting that you did. It's just in my profession. We always want to investigate why the mind works the way it does." Emily grimaced as she took offense to Paul's statement.

"So, you're suggesting that this is all in my head?" she yelled.

Paul, not prepared to handle the wrath of Emily's temper, digressed a bit. "I haven't reached that conclusion, but you have to understand that this profession doesn't entertain the notion of ghosts or any kind of paranormal activity. Also, if you don't mind, try not jumping down my throat every other question. Just because it's asinine to you doesn't mean it's not a valid question."

Emily began to gather her belongings to storm out of Paul Cusick's office and didn't care about the consequences. *The damn school board can fire me for all I care!* Not that it mattered as his office had nothing to do with her actual work benefits.

"What are you doing?" Paul calmly asked.

"If this profession doesn't and will not even consider that this may be happening to me, then why the fuck am I here? Hm? Tell me!" Emily yelled as she stormed towards the front door. She stopped and turned towards Paul with her hand on her hip. "Can you say that I am not out of mind?"

Paul folded his hands together and rested his chin on them. "No."

"If I am, is there anything that will make this go away?"

"No."

Looking away from Paul and towards the window in his office, she asked one more question, "Will I ever be the same person I was?"

Paul shook his head and answered, "No. But most people couldn't after a tragedy like this." Emily turned her back to Paul and shouted, "Then what the fuck are you even talking about? What's the damn point in this?" Emily looked down to the floor and breathed, "What's the point of anything now?"

Emily couldn't leave fast enough. Hiding from the ghastly children, she swung the door open and found them, waiting for Emily outside the office the entire time. They smiled at Emily, teeth chattering and arms reaching for her.

Collapsing to the floor, she started to feel cold, and as she gasped for breath. It felt like her lungs were freezing. Their eyes were now white all over except for a speck of blue in the middle.

All nine of the children put their hands in the air wanting Emily to take hold. Voices began to emerge from their chattering teeth, like whispers in her mind. "*C-c-come-come with usssss,*" the boy in the front said. Before, Emily thought their hair was white, but their hair was normal in color after looking closely. It was the frost and the ice that had formed on their heads that made it appear like they had no pigment.

The boy in front of her had a bullet hole in his chest and right arm. When he spoke again, it wasn't words that came out but the echoes of the moment he died. "*Noooo. Please! Don't!*" Even the sound of the shots fired came out of his mouth. Emily couldn't explain it, but she knew what happened from the boy's point of view. The boy put his arm up to shield himself and was shot, only to die from the other shot to the chest.

The girl next to the boy extended her hand to Emily as well, and when she opened her mouth Emily heard a sweet voice exclaim, *"Where do we go? What do we do! Help me! Help us!"* Then, the seven other children, grinning with smiles unnaturally stretching from ear to ear and teeth bigger than any child, or adult, should have, began to open their mouths. A crescendo of yells, screams, and pleadings of children began to flood Emily's ear canals. Her ears were on fire, and it burned so bad. She imagined it was how the shotgun blast felt when it drove into the skin. The more they seeped into her mind, the thicker the blackness around them became, almost engulfing them in darkness.

Kicking the door shut, Emily slid herself away from the door, and the noises stopped. The children's spirits were gone for now, but the dying echoes were still playing in her mind.

Paul watched from across the room to witness a woman terrified at something she had seen or thought she saw outside his front office door.

Emily caught her breath and turned her head to look at Paul. He appeared to be possibly confused but overly calm, given what he had seen with Emily screaming and falling. "There is nowhere to go," she said to Paul, "I am stuck in this office. They'll take me away if I leave this room."

Paul walked over to Emily, and as he looked down upon her, he asked, "Where is it you think they are going to take you?"

Emily had trouble mustering the words. After a few moments, with tears in her eyes, she replied, "Where I probably deserve to be. Hell."

4

The clock's tick tocks echoed throughout Paul's office. Paul made Emily lay down on the floor with a pillow for a while to help her relax. It may have worked as Paul detected a small snore from Emily in the half-hour that had passed. She had not slept in the past two weeks because she didn't feel like she needed to. It was almost like Emily was sleeping. She compared it to being asleep but still hearing everything happening in the area and then waking up pissed off because you slept terribly. Emily was drifting through life this past couple of weeks anyway. She had become accustomed to staying awake. Nothing seemed real. Caught in a perpetual nightmare of her own making due to what she believed was her fault, Emily accepted it as such.

"So, after the fight, what happened?" Paul asked, trying to get Emily's mind away from her thoughts.

At first, Emily didn't hear Paul as she did drift away for a moment. Before he spoke, Emily dreamt that she was caught in between life and something else. It was quiet in this area and unnatural as it was like looking out a window into the lives of others she had known and loved. The other side was like static on an old television set. Someone else was clicking through the channels of different landscapes; some of it was peaceful, some of it was terrifying. She could see a man in the dark hallway of her dream, but as the figure came closer, she saw that a television set was where his head should have been. On the screen was a picture of a sad clown face that looked like a small child had drawn it. Its head was too big for its body as the shape was tripping over its own feet from right to left, back to forth. The sounds of the television's channels being flipped through echoed through the hall. Each track had a different tragedy in the world. *"It's too much,"* a voice from inside the television said, *"I can't carry all this weight!"*

"Emily!"

"What?" Emily yelled, startled, as she sat up abruptly as if she were playing off the fact that she had fallen asleep.

5

Emily was perturbed. There was probably another word to describe her mood that evening, but that was what she kept thinking. Emily approached her building, where her apartment was, above the local antique store in town. She jammed her keys into the side door's keyhole. The ruckus woke up her landlord, Ms. Claire Dubois, from an afternoon slumber behind her cash register. Claire knew something was wrong. Emily's demeanor said it all.

"You look like you are about to burn thunder wood, dear. Is everything all right?" Claire asked.

Emily stopped and looked at her landlord, pushing and pushed back all the things she wanted to say because the older lady in front of her didn't deserve the hell fury that she could unleash. Emily threw her hands in the air and answered, "Yes. No. I don't know. You ever have a day where you just can't seem to win?"

Claire smiled and began to cool herself off using a Japanese hand fan in the shop. "Oh, yes, dearie," she replied, "But sometimes it's not all about you, love. Maybe it's finding a way to where everyone else wins and just be happy with that."

Emily stopped and thought about what she said and nodded, "Thanks, Ms. Dubois." Emily began to ascend the stairs in front of her.

"Call me Claire, girl! Ms. Dubois was my mother's name," Claire said before she realized Emily had gone upstairs to her apartment already. "Okay. We'll talk later, I suppose."

Crosby was in the extra bedroom in the apartment doing voice exercises to prepare to record his demo to send to agents. Moving his mouth around in strange positions while reciting the vowels, he didn't hear Emily storm through the front door. The walls shook from Emily violently closing the door. The coats and pictures hanging on the wall next to the entrance fell to the floor; this was a natural occurrence when Emily closed the door as she wasn't exactly delicate. One of the wall pictures was Emily and Crosby in front of a Ferris wheel in college. No matter how many times that picture fell, the frame that held it never broke or cracked.

Emily put down her purse and bag that contained her class's schoolwork. She walked down the small hallway and swung the door to Crosby's office open. Crosby, started by the sudden intrusion, slipped off his headphones and yelled, "Could you knock or something? What if I was recording something?"

Emily looked around and replied, "You're fine." She could not find what she was looking for as she scanned the room thoroughly

"Believe it or not, I may be able to help you. I mean, I won't tell your friends in the girl community that you needed a guy's help," Crosby said with an ounce of dry wit.

"Headphones."

Crosby looked back at Emily and said, "Come again?"

Emily walked around the room that seemed to change every time she walked into it continually. That's normal when someone is looking for something that they can't find; people tend to see items within an area they never noticed before. "You mentioned, at one time, you had a pair of noise-canceling headphones. Where are they?"

Crosby, confused, pointed to the closet and inquired, "I have a couple. Why do you need them?"

Emily swung open the closet door and replied, "I don't need both, at least not right now. Just the one would do." Emily pulled out the most expensive pair out of the two and asked, "Are the batteries still good?"

Crosby answered with a slight hint of concern, "Should be new ones in it, but, uh, I can't help but notice that you took the more expensive ones."

Emily turned around and shrugged her shoulders. "So?"

"It's just that those cost a lot. I hate to sound like my dad, but you shouldn't take those to school because they might get lost, stolen, or broken."

Emily nodded her head that indicated a sarcastic comment was on the horizon. "Oh, you mean this money suck that took away from our wedding fund. These overpriced pieces of plastic? Is that what you are referring to?"

Crosby was accustomed to this passive-aggressive song and dance that they had created together over the years. There wasn't a week that went by since the move to Marie-Glen that Emily hadn't brought up the fact they weren't married yet. He threw his hands in the air and said, "You know, there are nicer ways to get your point across."

Emily rolled her eyes and stormed out of the office into the living room.

"I love you, but all I'm saying is that one of us might need a bit of a nap!" Crosby yelled to get a smart-ass reaction he was used to from her. Emily was too focused on the idea that she had for her classroom to acknowledge his witty and insulting attempt; this was the couple's usual way of conversing with each other most of the time. It seemed that this would be unhealthy from an outside perspective. Still, it was something that they both laughed about later, regularly.

Determined, Emily didn't change out of her work clothes and instead found some drawing pads to plan a new arrangement and lesson plans. After about an hour of drawing and research on the internet, Emily's eyes began to grow tired.

Crosby emerged from his "Dude Dungeon" to see what his fiancée was up to. "What are you so involved with, babe?"

Emily shook her head and debated on whether to bother explaining her plight with her job. "I'm trying to find a way to get these kids to communicate in a meaningful way. How do you make kids that have seemingly nothing in common talk to each other? And if they are more alike than they think, how do I try to bridge that gap? Because of either being deaf, not knowing a different language, being too quiet, too outspoken, or even because they look different?"

Crosby, who was typically her rock, didn't have an answer. He didn't want to give a real solution that may have been wrong. The only thing he could do for Emily was to listen as best he could. "Sometimes, I wonder if we made a mistake coming here," she said, choking back her sadness. "It's too hard. I didn't think it would be this hard. This is the worst thing to happen so early in my career! How do they expect me to make this situation better? I am not ready for this. I am just a teacher barely hanging on to a terrible situation."

Crosby put his arm around her and glanced down at her notes, and put together what she was planning. His eyes grew big because he knew exactly what to say. It wasn't how to fix her problems in her profession; it was to put it in a way that fueled her ego that he knew needed a boost. "I don't think this is the worst situation for you. I think this is your golden opportunity and maybe the best thing that you may ever do." They both knew that it was tough being the first day and all, but Emily wasn't one just to wait; she wanted to solve it a problem now.

Both looked down at a table with a laptop, noise-canceling headphones, and a drawing paper that outlined a new seating arrangement.

6

After consuming more than a couple of cups of coffee in the teachers' lounge, Emily sat at her desk in the classroom, patiently waiting. Most teachers at Marie-Glen Elementary stayed in the room and conversed with one another. *A lounge? That's putting it nicely.* The breakroom was mainly an unused classroom with a couple of pleather couches that had been around since the early '90s. The couches had been sat in so much that the material was cracking, and the stuffing started emerging. It reminded Emily of when her brother and his friends went to sit on an old sofa that someone dumped in the middle of the woods, so they had a place to stash and read dirty magazines. As she got older, Emily wondered what kind of fluids were on that dusty old sofa and what an ultraviolet blacklight might find.

She never sat on the teachers' sofa because that memory caused her unjustified fear.

The school suspension for Brad Medler and Jamie Renee Cassidy ended this day. Emily was ecstatic about what she was about to unleash for her class and her standard curriculum. Nine o'clock came around, as students that their parents and the bus riders were dropping off started to occupy the halls. The first one in the class, as usual, was Sloane Chastain, the one that's a bit snobbish.

Upon entering the room at a brisk pace because she loved to be first, Sloane stopped immediately. She saw that the desks had moved from their usual locations. There was now a set of four rows of six directly placed next to one another in a horse-shoe shape. Sloane curled her upper lip and scoffed. Before she could get a word in, Emily said, "Your name is on the seat you are now assigned."

"But I liked the seat I had," Sloane whined.

"You'll get used to it… like most things in life," Emily replied with a smile on her face. "But!" Emily put her finger in the air to stop Sloane from going forward with her complaint. Her face was still smiling, if not a bit forced. "Please take your seat, Sloane."

Sloane stomped off to find her seat, which was on the right side of the horseshoe. After she sat down, the rest of the class started to come in, and they all had the same confused look on their faces that Sloane had. As they found their seats, Emily could hear the mumbling and the complaining, but it was going to get even better, at least for her.

At the time, her students didn't know that the new seating chart was strategic and based on their personalities and behaviors. Some may make a seating chart to make their lives easier for the eight hours they are working. Still, Emily was young, ambitious, and had nothing to lose in terms of her job. It was impossible to be one hundred percent perfect with this group of children. But the way Emily saw it was that no teacher is ever one hundred percent accurate.

Even though she had a little over twenty students, most of them were entirely able to learn but didn't necessarily want to. There were a select few that Emily felt needed more help, not because of their ability to learn necessarily, but more to these kids besides their probable learning disabilities. Emily wasn't entirely convinced yet that a handful of them had any learning disabilities per se. Jamie Renee was deaf, and Feng Song knew little English; that's not a disability but a hindrance.

It was clear from day one that Brad Medler and Derek Singletary didn't get along. Emily didn't think it was a race issue, but rather that they both wanted to be noticed but for different reasons. When one outwits another, jealousy set in; Brad wanted the laughs for validation. Derek just wanted an assurance in any way possible. They were assigned to sit next to one another in the back, where Emily had a direct sight.

The next set of students Emily decided to place together was known as the "Girl Trinity:"; Jamie Renee Cassidy, Ava Nauling, and Sloane Chastain. One was outspoken, one hardly spoke, and the other spoke mostly with her hands. They were all placed on the right-hand side of the class near the front.

Finally, Bo Gentry, the questionable one as Emily didn't know what his "deal" was, and Feng Song. There was no rhyme or reason to match up to them, but perhaps Feng could help Bo somehow. Then again, Emily wasn't sure that Bo needed any help at all, but maybe it could work vice versa. Feng was brilliant by all accounts, but his lack of knowledge regarding the English language affected his learning ability.

With a Cheshire Cat grin, Ms. Emily Sinclair stood up tall and announced, "We are going to do things a little bit different!" While Emily thought she was projecting the right amount of enthusiasm that she thought would be infectious to the students, the kids just found it disturbing. Since Emily started her teaching career with this classroom, she projected any contentedness, and the students knew it. She reached into the bottom drawer of her rusted desk and pulled out the pair of wireless headphones she had confiscated from Crosby and held them in the air.

"I realized that many of you don't realize how hard some people have it compared to others. So, what we are going to do is change what you are learning a bit!" Emily explained within jubilation. She held the headphones in both hands and started to move around the classroom as she told what she was planning.

"This is a pair of noise-canceling headphones with a fresh pair of batteries. As you all know, hopefully, Jamie is deaf. If you don't know what that means, I will explain it to you," Emily continued in a condescending tone. "That means she cannot hear. Nothing. Ever. So, what we will do each day is someone will wear these headphones and not hear as much. Now, these can't block all noise, so we will all have to be really quiet."

Brad was terrified that he was going to be the one that was going to wear the headphones. *I mean, why wouldn't he?*

Emily wasn't done, much to the students' surprise. She then walked back over to the overhead projector. She flipped it on to reveal a Japanese symbol with what it meant in English on top and how to pronounce it at the bottom: こんにちは or Kon'nichiwa, which meant "hello." "We are going to try to learn a new word each day in Japanese so Feng won't feel so left out and so he can learn more English words!"

"I thought we were going to learn Spanish because more people speak it in America?" shouted one of the male students."

Emily cut her eyes at him and replied, "You have all of high school to do that. We are going to broaden our horizons, Henry." Emily changed the sheet on the projector to a drawing of a woman making a hand gesture.

"Do you know what a universal language is?" Emily sincerely asked. There was a sudden silence that came over the class until Derek Singletary hesitantly raised his. Emily nodded to him, and he answered, "Is it a language that can be used all over the universe?" The class giggled at his answer. Jamie Renee concentrated the hardest she ever had before at what everyone was saying by watching their lips.

"Close! It is a language that can be learned that everyone can understand. Sign language is one, and maybe the only. I am not sure, to be honest. Jamie Renee knows sign language, so maybe we can learn some so we can talk to her a little more," Emily continued to explain. The class started to sigh at the potential work they were going to have to put in.

Emily sighed and leaned on her desk. *How do I make them understand?*

Being spoken down to all the time is what Emily, and probably most kids, hated growing up. She was a believer that sometimes the truth is what people, even kids, needed in life. Emily told herself that she wouldn't be the kind of parent that hid the many facets of living away from her children, so why should it be like that for her students?

"Every person wants to be included, kiddos. That's the truth. When you go outside to play, and no one wants to play with you, that makes you feel bad, right?" All the kids nodded their heads. "When you go to lunch, and you can't find anyone to sit with. That can be a little lonely, can't it?" Emily continued with examples the children agreed with. In contrast, some may say that there is nothing crueler than a child. Often, they have a higher capacity for empathy than most, and Ms. Sinclair's third-grade class would be an example of that.

"There will no longer be a single person in here that is left out. We all have the right to feel included in life, no matter how hard it is for us or anyone else. The truth is that we are not perfect, and sometimes some of us need to work harder, but that doesn't mean we have to make it harder than it needs to be. I am not asking anyone to be a perfect person because no one is; I just want you to be good ones. Cool?"

The responses did not all come at once. After a few moments, "Okay" and "Cool" were eventually spoken until everyone answered. Emily held up the headphones and menacingly smiled at Brad, knowing that he knew what was coming next.

"*Oh shit,*" Brad thought to himself.

Emily, grinning ear to ear, exclaimed, "You are the first prize winner to wear these bad boys. Now pay attention very closely because you are going to learn a few things." Brad huffed and slouched down in his seat. Derek laughed at his expense because he knew it was poetic justice. Brad cut his eyes at Derek, but it didn't deter him from finding humor. What Brad didn't notice was that the rest of the class was giggling, and what was the final nail in the coffin was when he looked over to his left to Jamie Renee. The girl he made fun of for being deaf was now grinning at him, knowing that he would have a hard day. Jamie felt bad for giggling, but she had to endure her disability every day. In contrast, Brad only had to be hard of hearing for about six hours.

"Give me your phone," Emily demanded. Brad's first inkling was to grab his bookbag decorated with band patches and run away. "Why?" he asked, genuinely not knowing the reason.

"You're a smart kid. Eventually, you or someone else will probably figure out that these are Bluetooth capable and that you can stream YouTube or music on it. I don't need that headache so pretty please, with sugar on top, let me have your phone until the end of the day."

As mad as Brad was that he had to give up what he thought was his entire life, he did gain an ounce of respect for the forward-thinking that his teacher, Ms. Sinclair, put in. "That goes for the rest of you as well," Emily said aloud. "The point of this is to try to imitate what it's like to lose one of your senses."

Emily then turned around back to Brad and whispered, "Make sure you pay attention."

Walking back to the overhead projector, Emily explained how "hello" was said in Japanese and then in sign language. When Emily asked the class to tell Feng "hello" in Japanese, everyone said "Kon'nichiwa" except for Brad. He yelled because he couldn't hear himself well. The class laughed, but

Brad, for the first time, didn't get mad. He knew that he was coming off as loud.

Emily then brought her hand to her left ear and then shifted it forward with her thumb near her head and her fingers pointed outwards. "That is how you say 'hello' with sign language," Emily taught. "Now practice that with the person to your left and right." All the students started to sign to one another, and for the first time, Jamie Renee's class signed in her language.

7

"So, you found a way to teach two separate languages at once, none of which are taught or even offered to be taught in most public schools," Paul said to Emily. She was now lying on the couch with her feet propped up. She figured that she wasn't going anywhere anytime soon, so she might as well get comfortable.

"Don't know that I would say that I found a way. I can't be the only person that came up with that idea. It's not like I was teaching whole sentences," Emily replied.

Paul got up to walk around because he started to become physically uncomfortable in his seat. He found an empty part of the wall and began to slam his back into it lightly. Emily didn't notice at first, but every time he threw himself against the wall, the impact became louder. The bookshelf next to him began to shake. The books organized on it began to move forward from the vibration.

Emily's eyes grew big as she realized what he was doing. She sat up and watched Paul, the man she trusted with her story and secrets as a therapist, threw himself against the wall as hard as he could only to watch the pain in his face.

Paul did not yell; he just grimaced until he felt the cracks in his shoulder blade areas. Emily heard the cracking of what she thought was Paul's spine and covered the bottom part of her mouth in shock at how loud it was.

"Are you all right?" Emily asked with genuine concern. Paul slowly walked back to his chair and replied, "It's fine. My body just starts to hurt if I stay in one kind of, um, position too long."

After letting out a sigh of relief once his rear hit the cushion of his old chair, Paul went immediately back into his usual therapist mode. Emily watched him as he sat down and opened his eyes back up, something different about Paul. There was an enticement in his eyes now—something that made you pay attention—something hypnotic. Paul peered at Emily, and for a moment, there was a light in his eyes that was beautiful. Emily shook her head and widened her eyes, so she could stay awake as she was sure she was hallucinating. Looking back at Paul, his face and eyes were normal again. *I just want to go to sleep forever.*

"Jamie Renee."

Emily snapped back into reality, or at least the truth that she was unwillingly becoming accustomed to. She sleepily replied, "Huh?"

Paul smiled and joked, "You are just smart as a tack right now, aren't you?"

Emily took offense to the joke as anyone could tell you, especially her fiancé, Crosby. She didn't like being the butt of the joke.

"Funny," Emily started, "I didn't realize the school district was so cheap that they hired a hack like you. By the way, the phrase is "sharp as a tack. "

Paul grinned as she was playing into his game.

"Oh, come on now, surely there is a sense of humor in there somewhere. I mean, how else could you make friends and such?" Paul inquired.

Emily stuck her nose in the air and looked down her nose at Paul and spoke. "How or what I do, or did, with my life isn't what I am here to talk about."

"I think it is," Paul replied. "It's how we deal with our insecurities. What are you so insecure about?"

Emily scoffed at Paul. The sheer arrogance that he suddenly seemed to unleash was staggering, but what Emily knew but never would admit was that he was right. "We grow up with all these preconceived notions about ourselves because we are molded to be in some way—from our parents, television, movies, friends, and so on. It's not who you are that holds you back; it's what you think you are not," Paul surmised. "That last sentence wasn't me. I read it somewhere."

"I am perfectly fine the way I am. I don't need validation from you or anyone else for that matter!" Emily yelled.

"Maybe not. Maybe it's when the other person that is not who you think they should be. I changed my persona just now, and you became defensive," Paul replied in a calm voice.

"I became defensive because you said I was insecure!"

"You're right. I'm wrong. Please tell me how I can do better," Paul said.

Emily stood up straight and began, "Well, I think you could actually listen instead of assuming, for starters. I didn't think that therapists were...." She stopped, realizing that she was proving Paul's point, but she was too stubborn to acknowledge it.

Paul then stuck his nose in the air and looked down his nose at Emily and said, "Right. Tell me why your fiancé left you."

Emily's eyes began to swell from attempting not to cry. Even in her situation, Emily still treated everything and everyone like a competition. She couldn't pinpoint where it came from, *probably from daddy like most women that walk into a shrink's office.* "That's not why I am here," she muttered.

"Then, why are you here?" Paul asked.

"Because there are dead children following me around, and if they are not around the corner, then there are others with black ink for eyes finding me and touching me. I can't sleep, and when I dodo, I wake up feeling more disconnected from this world than when I was last awake! There! That's it! Lock the loony bitch up with the padded cells because I'll always have somewhere to rest my head comfortably!" Emily stood up and paced around the office, wiping the tears as they trickled down her face.

"They touch you?" Paul asked.

"What?" Emily replied to Paul, confused.

"The kids. They touch you?"

She nodded her head and looked out the window on the other side of his office that just faced another building. "They try to, at least. Sometimes I swear that I can feel them, but maybe that is just wishful thinking in a way," Emily continued.

Confused, Paul asked, "How so? I thought they terrified you."

Emily nodded because she agreed with Paul's statement. "They do because I keep thinking that if I have contact with my students in their afterlife, they cannot move on. I think it scares me more that I don't know what is happening to them. Before, I could reach out to them as they could with me, but it's not like that now. Life is frightening enough; death shouldn't also be."

Paul hung on her words for a moment. He thought about everything that he had seen in his time and wondered what the last thoughts were before they died. Paul rubbed his face and then reached into his desk to pull out a pair of glasses because his eyes began to bother him. As he placed his spectacles on his face, Paul said, "You mentioned that Jamie was the first one you saw. When did this happen?"

Emily wiped away her cold tear as soon as they fell onto the back of her hands. Emily replied, "At the one place where I always felt safe…where no one would bother me too often when I needed to be by myself: the Johnson's Bookstore."

8

There was always something about the smell of a bookstore that put Emily and others at ease. It's still hard to pinpoint precisely what it was, but Emily knew deep down that it was a blend of different things. The terpene compounds that gave the books a wooden smell mixed with a sweet vanilla aroma aided in calm; Emily knew this and was convinced others did. The smell of coffee that came later when it became fashionable to put in a high-end coffee retailer added a sense of home in people's subconscious.

It was a week after the shootings, and Emily finally gathered up the courage to leave her home that was just as empty as she was. She told herself that if she were to make any progress and run away from her demons and the literal ghosts, it would be on her terms. There was no other place that she knew she would feel comfortable in than her favorite place in Marie-Glen: the Johnson Family Bookstore.

One of the great things about a thriving community is the population's dedication and the will to keep smaller businesses open. Even those who don't live in Marie-Glen would come because of word of mouth. With the name "Johnson" in the title, one would figure the store to have been around for generations, but it wasn't that old at all.

What made this bookstore different from the rest was its ability to keep enough stock of new and old novels without relying on a massive amount of square footage to hold it. Regardless of the popularity of digital books, the proprietor knew there was still a desire to keep a book physically.

The store's interior had an expensive cabin in the woods feel. The inventory consisted of books of every genre. If books were not on your shopping agenda, then perhaps a cup of affordable coffee and a pastry provided by a nearby bakery with a couple of friends would suffice with some friends. If children were around, then there was a small candy and soda bar, and if you were a good boy or girl, then maybe your folks would splurge for an actual root beer float. The key to the store's success was not the sales of literature but the sale of condiments, which was a higher markup. Deep down, the population of Marie-Glen knew this but never brought it up because they knew a good thing when they had it and knew well enough to leave it be.

The clacking sound started to enter to occur in the background of Emily's thoughts.

What the hell is that? she wondered. While the sound was a minor concern at the time, the sight of her students' faces haunting her and the recollection of events memories was more of a matter. For the last week, Emily had shut herself inside her apartment, waiting to see if she saw the ghosts of her class again; she hadn't. No communication with the outside world can take a toll on someone. Finally, Emily decided it was time to bring herself back into the world, at least for an hour or two. The news vans were no longer infesting the cobblestone roads of the town. It was safer for Emily to leave home without being bombarded with reporters and cameras. The media never knocked on her front door to their credit, which surprised Emily because film and television shows portrayed reporters as relentless.

Emily's home was cold. Every time she fiddled with the thermostat for the heat to turn on, she never felt it. *I thought I paid the heating bill. Maybe not.* But without another warm body next to her to keep her warm, what was the point? Crosby was gone, and there was no one else around to help her fill the void within her.

It's just down and across the street. I can do that for sure! Right? Why am I talking to myself like this? Emily sat up from the rocking chair that her grandmother willed to her when she passed. It was a safe place for Emily over the years. She did her best thinking there and had some of the best naps she ever had in that chair. With great determination, Emily walked through the door and walked down the hallway at a brisk pace before reaching the stairs.

As she reached the bottom, Emily saw her landlord and owner of the antique store below, Ms. Claire Dubois, or just Ms. Claire if you knew her personally. Claire comfortably sat in front of her cash register, with her elbow leaning against the windowsill with her hand resting her head. Emily stood and watched her friend and landlord, watching the world continue outside while she stayed indoors. She seemed sad, and Emily wasn't sure if she were the person that could help her feel better. *I'm not.* Emily was sure she wasn't.

Emily made her way towards the door that led to the other side of the building, the door she and Crosby used to get inside. Otherwise, they would have to go through the store all the time, and Ms. Dubois never left the door unlocked after she left for the day.

"It must be lonely for you," Claire said softly.

Emily poked her head back through the threshold of the store from the back. She wasn't sure if she talked to her or if Miss Claire may have finally started to go senile.

"You haven't left yet," Claire stated.

Emily walked back into the building and the store and addressed her.

"I was just going to try to get out for a bit," Emily explained.

Claire turned her head slightly to acknowledge her presence. Claire forced herself not to look straight at Emily but felt the need to get something off her chest.

Emily leaned in to look at Claire's eyes, but she moved her head in another direction. *Why doesn't she want to look me in the face?*

"You need to go, dear. There is no need for you to stay here alone. All you will accomplish is retaining the loneliness that you keep in your company," Claire said, clenching her jaw.

Emily backed away from Ms. Dubois as she cut her eyes toward her.

"You've done enough! Just go!" Claire yelled, scaring Emily to run outside. It wasn't a hateful yell, but more of a concerning one. Maybe even a shout from a sadness deep down inside. From the outside of the store, Emily continued to listen to Claire, crying, "Why? Nothing good will come of this! Please just go!"

Emily quickly placed her hands over her ears to drown out the yelling as she began to break down again. She didn't want to hear it. It was not because she was sensitive, but because Emily was attempting not to acknowledge what she already knew; Emily was a failure because she couldn't save them. *I don't know if she is trying to help or make me feel worse. It sounds like she hates me.*

Claire became silent, and Emily, with a tear-stained face, sighed with relief. She took her hands and slowly lowered them to her side cautiously, waiting for the screams of an old woman to happen again. When the echoes of the hall fell silent after the door closed behind her, Emily opened her eyes.

She realized that her landlord had started glaring out the window towards her. Emily took a deep breath and looked down the road from around the corner of the building. If anyone saw her at this moment, it would look like she was spying on someone. *It's not that far. I mean, not that many people will see me.* That one thought made Emily realize that it wasn't the media she was afraid of; it was everyone else.

As Emily walked past the shop window, she looked at Claire from the corner of her eyes and saw that she was talking to herself on the other side of the glass. She watched Claire's mouth the words, *"You can only do so much."*

Walking down the sidewalk, Emily looked at every person that walked by her through the corners of her eyes. No one seemed to recognize her. No one paid much attention. Emily was confused; on the one hand, she was a bit relieved, but on the other hand, she could entertain the thought that people had gone back to normal already. Like shootings just happen, and then they just go on with their lives. *It's not fair! I wish to be like everyone else.* But Emily was not like everyone else; she was there and witnessed more than any person should have to bear.

A few minutes of a peaceful walk through part of downtown to the Johnson's Bookstore, which she so admired, helped clear some of her worries and insecurities. Emily noticed that she used to smell the coffee from outside that reminded her of home, but now she couldn't. She took a hard sniff and got a slight Hazelnut scent; it wasn't much, but it was enough to be satisfied with for a moment.

Walking through the store's front doors seemed surreal; everything looked the same, but it didn't feel the same. Every time Emily walked in, there was always a feeling of joy that went through her body. Now there was nothing but a sense of emptiness. She couldn't even enjoy the store's smell like before because she couldn't smell anything substantial. *Is there nothing left? Do I just exist now with nothing I can, or want to, latch on to? But I smelled coffee! Why? That was probably my mind tricking me by association. I just want to feel something again.*

Emily moved through the store, and the aisles of books that she could have spent hours looking at felt like a chore more than an escape now. Everyone around her seemed to move at a slower pace, or perhaps she did. Emily heard a quiet melody of children singing as all other sounds became muted in her mind. She slowly looked around and turned her attention to the little children singing "The Itsy-Bitsy Spider."

Emily looked slightly to the right and saw a familiar silhouette reading a book with their back turned to her.

"...went up the waterspout."

Walking up to the child at a steady pace, Emily couldn't believe who it possibly was. *No. It's impossible. It can't be.* But she could pick her out of a crowd. Her hair was always down and tucked behind her ears that protrude a bit, but more than that, it was how she carried herself. She never stood up straight when doing a task. A bent knee and the tilt of the head to the right was a dead giveaway.

"Down came the rain..."

Emily came up right behind her and started to put her hand on the girl's shoulder. She didn't want to startle Jamie because she couldn't hear anything coming up behind her. *It can't be you, Jamie Renee. I saw you...."*

Putting her hand to her side and moving it up and down to get her deaf student's attention, Emily began to feel some warmth in her body. In her soul. She was so confident it was Jamie. The child brought her head to an upright position noticing the hand next to her.

"...and washed the spider out."

Everything that was going on around her started to silence itself; the cappuccino machine, the cash registers, the talking amongst friends, even the children's singing begun to fade away. The little girl slowly turned her head around, and the shape of her face began to show.

"Out came the sun that dried up all the rain…."

The child swung her whole body around toward Emily. *It's her! Oh my God, it's her!* It was Jamie Renee, but not like she remembered her. Jaime's face looked white…*white as a ghost.* The darkness highlighted Jamie's imperfections on her face, creases, and dents, but her eyes were the blackest of all.

Emily put her hands up, wanting to touch her face, but she was scared to touch the darkness around her. Billowing smoke emanated from her body, and the blackness of her eyes began to trickle down her face like tar. "What happened? What's been done to you?" Emily whimpered, wanting so badly to embrace the child here in front of her. Jamie's mouth opened, and a deafening cry echoed through Emily's mind. The blackness that swam in her eyes began to pour out heavier the more she cried. The black tears fused onto the darkness the surrounded her before they ever hit the floor. The blackness was Jamie's sadness growing as every tear shed turned into the black smoke around her.

As Jamie cried, the children that were reciting nursery rhymes looked at Emily with a confused stare. Emily looked around in terror as everyone in Johnson's Family Bookstore began to stare at her. Finally, bringing her hands to Jamie's ghostly face, Emily tried to wipe away the black tears from her face with little success. "W-wh-WHY!" Jamie screamed with a slight lisp. Emily backed away from her quickly, looking at the blackness on her hands as it appeared to spread around them. Closing her eyes and trying to find her voice, all Emily could say was, "I-I-I don't know! I'm sorry! I don't know why you're here! So sorry…I…am…so sorry I couldn't help you!"

When she realized that she was running away from one of her students that she adored, others rushed towards Jamie. The customers began rubbing on her like she was being worshiped, and all Emily could do was walk back to her. Jamie stepped back as Emily started to move forward again. As Jamie shrieked, the men and women turned around and stared Emily down.

"Let me help," Emily softly requested, "I failed before, but let me try. Let me help you! Tell me what to do! Tell me how to save you!"

Jamie put her hands over her spectral ears and began to hum with her eyes closed. Emily knew that she was no longer wanted and ran out the door of Johnson's Family Bookstore in fear of being accosted by a swarm of angry residents. When she looked down at her hands, she noticed that the black substance had disappeared. Confused, Emily looked to her right and left to see if anyone had noticed her, but no one did. At that moment, she realized that she would never go back to her favorite place again because the people of Marie-Glen wouldn't want her to.

Not anymore.

The Hindrance &
The Heartache

"I'm kind of interested in the two boys. The ones you made sit next to each other that didn't appear as they'd get along," Paul said, after hearing about Emily's first spirit encounter.

All Emily could think about is how odd it was that someone would go directly into another conversation so quickly after hearing that; *Really? That's what you're thinking about right now?*

Emily raised her finger to point out the peculiarity of the question after the fact. Instead, she decided to let bygones be bygones and continue the session the way Paul Cusick felt fit. "Are you talking about Brad Medler and Derek Singletary?"

"Yes!" Paul exclaimed, "I am always fascinated by people who are seemingly different in a small space."

Emily grinned at Paul's ignorance of popular culture, "You pretty much just stated the premise of almost every reality show in existence."

Paul grimaced at the notion and explained, "I don't really watch television."

Emily's eyebrows raised, and while she wasn't surprised, she couldn't relate; she loved her stories.

"You seemed surprised," Paul pointed out.

"No. Not at all, actually. But for someone who claims to love seeing human interaction, it's a little strange, I suppose."

"Why do you love it?" he asked.

Emily wondered if she wanted to go down this road. "Look," Emily began, "If you're like me and think that humanity is terrible, then television and film are your escape, even if just for an hour or two." Emily began to speak again but cut herself off.

Paul squinted and pointed out, "You were going to continue that thought?"

Emily shook her head and replied, "Yes. But if you never get into that type of thing, you probably wouldn't understand."

Paul welcomed the challenge by saying, "Try me."

She accepted his challenge. "Film, for me, shows us history in the eyes of someone else. It shines the light on humanity in ways that are lost on us and make us feel better. They challenge our minds with the complexity of their plots and can make someone who feels lost a little bit better by seeing that it can be. That's why I like film."

Paul nodded his head and then proceeded to move on.

"So, the two boys. How did that work out in the end?"

2

It was true. Derek Singletary and Brad Medler were nothing alike—from their speaking, ways of thinking, and even skin tone. However, it is human psychology, nature, and to include ourselves in others' lives that feel familiar to our own.

Emily pulled the short straw on chaperoning third-grade recess after lunch for one week; if her kids were not enough of a job, she had to keep up with three other classes at the same time. *It wouldn't be so bad if they were sitting down, but a bunch of kids running around being obnoxious was something else.* The girls were fine. The boys, on the other hand, were terrors.

Derek Singletary was the one exception to the rules, though. Every day that week, Emily would watch him go from group to group, trying to get involved with whatever game the other boys were playing. They would quickly dispatch and leave Derek alone, wondering. It wasn't because the other boys didn't like him; they didn't understand him. Derek was on a higher maturity level than the rest. That much was obvious, but his lack of understanding of simple mathematics and writing was the reason he was in Emily's class. He was proper, polite, and patient about his shortcomings. Still, as many people know, there is only so much a person can take before it comes to a head.

Sitting on the bench against the school's brick exterior, Emily watched Derek's final straw. The boys he wanted to hang out with were not doing anything in terms of playing. Still, when Derek suggested playing a pretend game, they all shook their heads in disagreement. Frustrated, Derek walked away and found a spot on the ground located under a dome that the kids could crawl through to sit and cry to themselves.

Brad Medler had caught wind of what was happening from across the playground. He was never the type that appeared to care more about anything than his wit and popularity. Something spoke to Brad that day when he saw Derek's loneliness. Emily had put them next to one another with her seating chart. While the two, at first, didn't particularly care for one another, they remained civil to each other; they helped each other when they could and had conversations about different topics: anime, movies, comics, and so on.

As Brad left the group, Emily watched as he left his other friends to walk over to where Derek went to hide. There was hesitation in his steps as he grew closer, but something in Brad that day, despite his ego and own childish narcissism, made him feel bad for Derek.

Brad leaned over the dome's opening and found Derek balled up with his head buried in his knees, trying to hide his sadness. Brad took a deep breath and asked, "You okay?" Derek lifted his head, not expecting to find Brad standing over him. He wiped his eyes and replied with some disdain, "What do you care?"

Brad smirked and explained, "I don't know. Maybe because I think everyone should have a good time during recess, ya know?"

Confused, Derek looked at him and admitted, "It's weird. I never thought you would be the one to be all concerned about me."

Brad smiled, and with his comical smugness, replied, "Yeah. I surprise even myself sometimes."

Derek shook his head and rolled his eyes at Brad's ego. Brad extended his hand to help Derek up. Derek took Brad's pale white hand and looked at Brad's freckled face and short black hair as he stood. Brad didn't have to take an interest, but he did, and sometimes that is all it takes to make someone's life better, if even for a moment.

"What do you want to play?" Brad asked as they emerged back onto the playground, where others could see.

"I want to play "Spies, " Derek answered.

Brad thought about it for a moment and had a single question, "How the hell do you play that?"

Derek's face lit up as he began to explain. "You have to see if you can catch other people's conversation, but you have to do it without being on the ground a hundred percent of the time."

Brad's face clenched up as he gave it some thought. "Isn't that just a more complicated version of eavesdropping with a mix of playing Lava?"

Derek became confused as he had never heard of the Lava game. "I don't know what that is."

Brad cut his eyes at Derek, and in a monotone yet annoying voice, asked, "You don't know what Hot Lava is?"

Derek shook his head and shrugged his shoulders.

"How have you lived your childhood, man? How have you never played Lava?" Brad continued.

Derek smirked and replied, "By not playing Lava, I guess." It was a right enough answer.

Brad shook his head in disbelief and simply said, "You're killing me, man."

Emily never thought much of it then. After talking to Paul about why films consumed her, she realized she was witnessing a feel-good moment occur in front of her. She never thought anything of it before because it wasn't on screen encased in a rectangular box. Paul managed to point out there is right in his way, and it usually happens more than we think; Emily's recollection of this moment was proof of it. Derek Singletary and Brad Medler became the most unlikely partners in crime as the months went on. *Touché, Paul, touché.*

3

Thunk-thunk-thunk.

There was someone in Emily's apartment. Emily dreamed of the celestial forest that she had been dreaming about for the last couple of nights since she awoke to the circle of dead children watching her. Each time she had sunk deeper into the forest soil with its red sky and oddly colored trees, she had felt at peace. She wanted to be absorbed by the dirt for eternity, so she could escape the images and anxiety that now plagued her thoughts.

The light sounds of whispering began to pull her out of her dreamscape and back into reality. She heard steps in the hallway subconsciously. Her eyes began to move back and forth behind her closed eyelids, trying to wake herself up. *Is she in there?* The voice was familiar to her, but she couldn't place it. The adolescent voice was rather deep and full of dread.

Thunk-thunk-thunk.

A pair of footsteps were coming from her hallway. The creaking of her hallway closet door finally woke her from her slumber. *Watch her. She needs to know.* Not precisely putting together what was happening inside her home, Emily sat up with her eyes still shut. There was a faint yelp of fright and trepidation coming from the end of the bed. Emily opened her eyes and saw a tall boy with big white eyes, different from the others with deep black eyes and long fingers holding on to the end of the footboard.

"Don't scream," the young man demanded as his mouth leaked black plasm.

Emily put her hands over her mouth to keep from frightfully yelling. Papers were being shifted around in the other room. He was not alone.

Mumbling under her hand, Emily told it to "Get out."

The dark figure's eyes grew more extensive, and his mouth began to open, releasing black smoke. "Get out," Emily whispered as she uncovered her mouth.

I'm done.

The voice in the living room was deep and distorted, like the ghost in front of Emily. There were two of them.

"Leave me alone! Get out!" Emily finally shouted. The boy's eyes began to swell up with milky white tears. Emily knew those tears, the way they formed; she saw them that day on the playground. She was looking at Derek Singletary's apparition in front of her.

Derek did not yell back. He didn't approach her. His stuttering voice simply said with an echo, "I'm sorry. I'm sorry we didn't do better that day."

Emily stood up, determined to get her former students out of her home, to keep them from plaguing her life. All she wanted was to forget, but they were a constant reminder that she failed them.

Another ghostly figure emerged from the side of her bedroom door. The being was a shorter boy with white freckles that stood out over his black visage. Please don't be mad. We didn't want this. The voice was different, but his sentence's inflection told Emily that Brad Medler was also in her home. They brought the children's sounds, yelling and screaming that day that lingered in the air like a soundtrack to her endless nightmare. Emily looked around to see if that day had come back to her to drive her insane. She expected to see all the children attempting to run out of the classroom that day, but it was nothing but the sounds of a nightmare entering her ears.

"Get! Out!" Emily screamed.

Both boys quickly floated away, leaving traces of black smog in her bedroom and out into the hallway.

"It's not my fault! If you got up and left into the other fucking room like I told you, you could have made it!" Emily hurtfully yelled as she walked out of her bedroom violently. Her front door swung open, and she heard footsteps leaving her home but saw no trace of the two boys. The door slammed shut.

Emily violently opened the door and looked down the hallway to find them. She wasn't sure what she would do, but Emily felt darkness inside her like she had never known before. Emily wanted to hurt something. She only felt that way after waking up from her dreams. She was becoming cold and callous. I just want to feel alive again.

After calming herself, she walked back into her living room and walked down the hall. Emily noticed that her closet door was hanging open. Thoroughly inspecting it, she saw that her box of student and teacher memories had disappeared. Emily was always one for nostalgia. She had a box of pictures stored in her closet. Items like old letters from high school, photos, and anything that the class gave her as a present, the memories that she liked.

She slowly turned her head back toward the living room. Scattered pieces of paper and greeting cards were lying on the floor. She followed the scattered memories trail, picking up each one as she went until she reached the living room.

Emily collapsed onto her knees. She saw her students' cards and artwork made for her lying in the middle of her living room. They reminded her of the children that she had lost on the day of the incident. Yellow, blue, and white construction paper with stick figures and other types of drawing meant to encapsulate Emily's essence hung open: some with rainbows, some with a drawing of the other kids, and even some with a spaceman. However, all of them were addressed to Emily as "Ms. Sinclair." Each one of them had the name of the child who created it. Not all of them were older paintings and sketches, though, as some of them were new. Emily had seen these pieces before.

They were all from that day. It was art day in the class on October 15th, and it was what her class was working on when the shots echoed down the hall. Emily was always looking forward to what the children would come up with as she let their imaginations go and translate to the paper.

Emily, frail and sobbing, cried onto a dusty hardwood floor over the memories that she had collected over time but no longer wanted. She realized that she came off like a monster to the very kids she vowed to teach and have patience. They don't know any better. They are clinging onto something in this world and not passing it on, and that person is me. Emily was sure of it. I should have died.

As Emily stood back up, her sobbing stopped as she looked on the ground and collected colored papers and saw that it spelled out a message to Emily…

WE SEE YOU

The One Up Lady

It took a significant amount of mental energy to tell her therapist, Paul Cusick, about her first real, physical, paranormal experience. Emily was never one to believe in spirits, demonic possession, or poltergeists. Then again, she had never been around death before—not like this. The ticking of the old clock in Paul's office echoed through the room. *What do you say after that?*

She had to take a break. There was only so much that Emily could talk about in chunks of time; she didn't want to throw out too much information and overload Paul's brain. Just then, Emily had a strange fantasy of Paul's face melting off after unleashing a barrage of crazy on him like in Raiders of the Lost Ark.

What should I say? Emily asked herself. Paul looked up at her from his notes on his lap as if he had heard her. *Did I just say that out loud?* She needed an ice breaker of sorts, and maybe talking about the event and the impact it had made on people would be good.

"Do you want to hear a pick-up line?" Emily asked Paul.

Paul crinkled his nose, trying to loosen his glasses from sticking to it. He smiled and thought about the last pick-up line he heard from someone and how much he laughed at it. As he recalled, it was something to the effect of, "If I were a battery and you were a potato chip, I would be Eveready, and you'd be Frito-Lay."

"Color me intrigued," he smiled.

Emily smiled with one side of her mouth, knowing that Paul was expecting a colorful anecdote. She quickly replied, "You won't laugh. At least if you are halfway human. If you do find it funny, then at least hide it because it's not funny, at least to me."

Now Paul was more interested than before as he sat up in his chair. "I think I can act a bit more human than you may think. I've been playing the part for a while now."

Emily looked around as if someone were spying on her and proceeded with the "clever" pick-up line she had heard in public: "Damn girl, are you a school? Because I would like to shoot some kids up in ya."

She put her hand over her mouth, not believing what she had just said out loud. All Emily wanted to do was change the subject a bit but instead spread a terrible joke to someone else. "I can't believe I just told you that," Emily said, ashamed of herself.

Paul leaned back in his chair with a disappointed look. "Where did you hear that?" he asked. Emily shivered at her own words and answered, "Some teenagers that I overheard talking as I was walking to the store."

The most important question that a shrink will ask, surprise no one, was uttered: "And how did that make you feel?"

Really? Emily crossed her arms defensively like she had to justify what she just said. "When I first heard those words uttered, it took a minute to process. After a minute, I was disgusted about how easy it was for people, maybe even the world, to brush it off so soon as something that is supposed to be normal. What bothered me more was thinking about it. If I were not a part of what happened at the elementary school, I am not sure that I wouldn't have chuckled at the joke at some point. Does that make me a bad person?"

"Do you think that makes you a bad person?" Paul asked.

Emily balled up her right fist and slammed it on the arm of the chair in anger. "Enough of the psychoanalytical bullshit!"

Paul didn't flinch as this was not the first ounce of rage he had encountered. He had gotten this reaction from others he had tried to help.

"I came here for answers, goddammit, so just give them to me!"

Emily knew that she overreacted and was immediately embarrassed by her lashing out. Paul slid his glasses over the tip of his nose and asked, "You realize that I am not a parapsychologist, right?"

Looking away, Emily nodded her head.

"What do you think you are going to get out of this session?" Paul asked.

Emily shrugged her shoulders and replied, "I don't know. I think I just want to know that I am not the only one that this has happened to. I want to know that I will recover, and the ghosts will go away over time and that everything will be all right in the end."

Clack-clack-clack.

The sound was back and louder than ever. Emily looked around the room to see the lighter-colored ghosts of children she didn't know when they lived. The room started to spin, and Emily put her hands over her ears to drown out the noise. She felt a hand touch her arm, and as she began to pull away, she saw it was Paul trying to calm her down.

The sound of chattering teeth began to fade, and Paul, with compassion in his eyes, said, "It's okay. Everything will be all right."

Emily shook her head, hoping to rid her mind of the sounds from beyond. With a sigh, she asked, "Is that your professional opinion?"

Paul smiled and answered her question with another in typical form. "Does it matter?"

"Probably not, but thanks for saying so."

2

"I'm curious," Paul began a new conversation, "You talk about the children you taught for about a year and a half but haven't mentioned any of the other teachers you worked with. Surely you became acquainted with a few of them."

Emily reflected for a moment about her times in meetings and hanging out in the teachers' lounge at Marie-Glen Elementary and the people she came across and realized that she didn't socialize much.

"I'm kind of strange," she replied, "I have always found it hard to connect with other people most of the time. This vicious circle of me wanted to be myself, but then knowing that my personality was quite different from many other people around me. Then I would shut myself off in fear of being ostracized by others."

Intrigued, Paul started writing in his journal, and as he finished, he took his glasses off. At this point, Emily knew Paul's routine. When he was interested in a subject, he took his glasses off. Still, when it was the usual song and dance of the "cray-cray" that Emily was undoubtedly displaying, he put his glasses on.

"So, then, it would be safe to say that you have some anxiety?" Paul asked.

Emily chuckled and replied, "Not at all. In fact, I would say that I have a lot of anxiety, especially now."

Paul thought about her social anxiety and asked, "Then why is it so much easier to talk to kids than adults?"

Emily looked to the ceiling to concentrate on the right answer she knew wouldn't come across well anyway. "Have you ever noticed that when a child tells an adult the truth about the way things are, they are considered cute? But when adults express themselves the same way they come across as an ass-hole?"

Paul wasn't entirely sure because he had never worked with kids before, but he agreed with Emily anyway. "I think that telling the truth brings the child into what you are saying more than simply tiptoeing around the issue. I appreciate that. Educating children was easier because adults tend to resist learning more. After all, it can impose on their personal beliefs. Being wrong, even for a short time, is never an option nowadays. I am not a person that takes an easy shortcut. I say what needs to be said, and it may be wrong sometimes, but that—I think—keeps me isolated from others."

Paul liked her answer and committed it to memory as best he could. "Tell me about the people that you did connect with and maybe even the ones you didn't."

Emily appreciated the escape, even if for a small amount of time. She grinned and said, "Margie Furlong and Jamison Harris. I think as a trio, we were probably the goofiest of the lot."

3

Emily would never forget the day she conversed with the rest of the staff of Marie-Glen Elementary. Most of the team regarded her as the quiet one, the mysterious one. The woman loved talking about her. The few men in the school loved to fantasize about her. To be fair, a couple of the women romantically thought about her as well.

It was the beginning of the second month of Emily starting her full-time teaching career. What that usually meant was the arrival of the monthly school supply catalog, The Ocean Side School Specialty. This monthly occurrence was the highlight of the break room during the children's lunchtime, and it was a tad asinine. No one can trace it back to when it started. Still, year after year, all the teachers would look through the catalog. Even with the school district providing the usual supplies or pencil sharpeners, staplers, and pens, this book of teacher supplies put their "cheap" supplies to shame. Then one teacher, at some point, would buy a product. Not because it was needed, but because the others would be in awe of that person for a while until someone else bought something new and fabulous. If you can call the teacher supplies fabulous, that is. According to Emily and a few others, this was the equivalent of a high school popularity contest, only sadder.

Not only did you have regular supplies, but you also had arts and crafts supplies included inside the catalog. The teachers have had full discretion on what they did with their students as far as creativity is concerned. The products from the catalog were, at the very least, a huge inspiration for them. There were a couple of unspoken rules when ordering.

First, a faculty member had to indicate that they bought something that was an upgrade from what they had beforehand, making sure that no one attempted to copy another teacher.

Second, if you were going to order arts and crafts from the catalog, you would make sure another teacher could not already do that theme. Two classrooms with the same look would be *"Totes embarrassing,"* as Emily would say, mocking today's culture.

Third, you could only spend so much on an item. After all, they're teachers, and if everyone could agree on something, it's that teachers don't get paid nearly enough anyway. The teacher's spending limit was a hundred dollars for one item, which was still too high. However, there was a loophole that was never brought to light or even talked about. A teacher by the name of Rachael McKay exploited it.

Rachael McKay. That stuck-up, self-tanning lotion-obsessed, one-upping bitch.

Emily didn't care what anyone said: "There is a fake person in every group, and they were usually named Rachael." *Pffft, Rachael. If there was a cancerous lump in my body, I would name it Rachael because it would be annoying like her and probably just as oddly colored.* Many of the staff believed that insects flew into Rachael's nose because it was stuck in the air more times than not.

To be fair, most of the contempt was more jealousy and envy than anything else. Rachael was the youngest teacher in the school. She didn't exactly have the same level of professionalism that the other teachers had. For example, Rachael's shirt was unbuttoned down to the full extent, revealing her cleavage. She was a hit with the fifth-grade boys and the male staff, along with a couple of women. She was attractive as well, which made it all the easier to hate her. *Rachael? What's with the extra "a" in her name anyway? If that doesn't say pretentious, I don't know what does.*

Like clockwork, when the new catalog showed up in teachers' mailboxes, so did their orders from the previous month. Like clockwork, all the teachers brought theirs in to show off. Emily's first account of the legendary "Office Supply Showcase" happened this day, and all she could do was sit back and watch the show.

First up was Mrs. Krisinski, a second-grade teacher, who sauntered into the teachers' lounge with a box in hand and a silly walk to boot. Emily had never seen anyone so happy about receiving office supplies before. It was the equivalent of watching a child jump up and down in anticipation of opening a gift. All the rest of the teachers gathered around as she laid the box on the nearest desk. Handshaking, Mrs. Dana

Krisinski told everyone, "I have been saving up for this for a while now, and I never thought I would get it."

"You're not giving your Oscar acceptance speech. Just open the box already!" a voice from the back of the room blurted. Emily shifted her gaze to Jamison Harris, another second-grade teacher whose classroom was adjacent to Krasinski's. They didn't hate each other, but they grinded each other's gears quite frequently.

"Oh, shut up, Jamison! I think you might be a little jealous," she replied.

Jamison swallowed the coffee in his mouth and quipped, "Yes. How can I ever live my life without spending an absurd amount of money on something that someone else already provides?" Jamison was the sarcastic type.

Dana just shooed him away with her hand and proceeded to open the box with a used butter knife she saw on the counter.

If there were ever a time when a radiant beam of light could come down to glorify the box displayed, that would have been the perfect time to show all its cardboard glory. The rest of the teachers' lounge teachers, beside Emily, Jamison, and another teacher, investigated the box, waiting for the mystery item's reveal. As Dana Krisinski buried her hands in the packing peanuts to find the package within, she slowly brought her hands up to present a stapler, but not just any stapler. It was a black Swingline Portable Electric Stapler with a push-button operation for easy staple loading and the ability to staple up to twenty sheets of paper at a time. It had red trim and was perfect.

There were whispers within the group, and as Dana listened, there was instant gratification. She would be the school's talk for at least a couple of days and had a new toy that may, or may not, make her life more comfortable. Mrs. Dana Krisinski was on top of the world, but then Ms. Rachael

McKay came into the room with a slightly bigger box. *Rachael, the proverbial itch on my crotch.*

With her nose in the air, Rachael announced her arrival with a fake smile and chirpy attitude. *Funny how nice she was when she wanted something like attention.* All the staff whipped their heads around to see Ms. McKay and her young beauty, holding another box from Ocean Side School Specialty. They knew because of the stenciled wave logo that the company printed on its packages with bright Persian blue ink. Dana saw this box. Her smile fell to a frown immediately. Rachael may have blown past the value of her. *Blown it out of the water* in a childish game of "Whose is better." The likelihood of that happening was high. Rachael was single and still living off some of her father's money after college, which allowed her to live a bit more extravagantly than her peers.

Rachael set her box down on another table far away from where the group had congregated and said, "I am so excited about what I got y' you all!" They didn't want to cave because of how Rachael presented herself. The group focused on Dana Krisinski for a moment. They then shifted their gaze towards Rachael and her bigger container of goodies.

"I can't wait to try these out!" Rachael squealed like a child as she reached into the box. The only thing Dana had running through her mind was, "These? In other words, more than one item in the box?"

Rachael pulled out the first item very slowly to purpose-fully create some dramatic effect in the room. It was another stapler but in a giant box. On the outside, it appeared to look like a regular stapler. But when you look at the specifications, it was one of the most advanced staplers on the market: the Novus B8FC Plat Clinch Power on Demand Executive Stapler.

There were actual gasps in the small crowd, almost orgas-mic, as they came to realize what it was. The B8FC was the crème de la crème of staplers. It featured the industry's only Power on Demand (POD) and required seventy percent less effort to staple *because regular stapling took so much energy.* It could also staple up to fifty sheets of paper at once and merely touch the orange button on the top for "one-touch" stapling. Emily wondered if she realized that she taught in an elementary school. In no way would she ever need to staple five sheets of paper at once, much less fifty.

"That stapler is a hundred and twenty dollars," Dana yelled from the end of the room. She needed to be loud in a group to get the most attention, which was obnoxious for the rest of the teachers. Glares of indignation came from some of the staff, but they were fascinated with the stapler not to act pleasant.

Rachael grinned as she pulled her attention away from her new stapler. She knew the rules but found that loophole that no one ever had used before this day. "You're right, Dana, it is. You got me!" Rachael said.

Dana nodded her head as she proudly accused her rival of breaking the rules that no one ever really wrote down.

"But," Rachael continued, "it was on sale last week online, and I just had to have it because it was $90!"

Appalled, Dana didn't have the words to belt out when she wanted. After a moment, all Dana could put together was, "Online? You mean you didn't order from the catalog?" *This is my moment, goddammit!*

Rachael put down the box her new, *overpriced* stapler came in onto the table and condescendingly smiled at Dana before replying, "Catalog? No. Sorry, sweetie, but I'm not sixty years old. I use the internet."

She did this on purpose! She waited for people to order and then waited for it to go on sale just so that she could pay for the fast shipping to make sure it came in on time so she could show me up! What a bitch! Dana thought, convincing herself that it was right as she didn't have a reason to think otherwise.

While that may seem a bit excessive, it was the truth. Rachael played the waiting game where she could receive all the attention for that one day, that one moment. She wanted people to pay attention to her. She craved it, but the dirty little secret was that everyone else craved it as well.

Rachael reached back into the box to reveal a set of scissors. To the untrained eye, they would appear to be ordinary scissors. They weren't.

They were the Acme Non-Stick Scissor, 8 in, Titanium Blade scissors, the best pair of scissors on the market right now, and they were the sharpest and most sturdy. "Oh, I like those scissors!" and "Those are worth the money" were phrases uttered amongst the other teachers.

Rachael McKay had won the popularity contest for the month. As the teachers went back to educate their students, Dana Krisinski walked beside Rachael. With hate deep in her voice, Dana whispered, "I hope those titanium scissors fall off your desk and stab you in the crotch, you conceited twat."

Rachael didn't respond and didn't understand the anger toward her. It was all a bunch of old bitties getting their bloomers in a bunch as far as she was concerned. All she wanted was to be unique for a day, where others would talk to her, but no one else realized that and based it all on how she carried herself.

Emily still had a few minutes left because her class was not far from the lounge than the other school rooms. The only people left in the place were Emily, Jamison, and Margie Furlong. Ms. Margie Furlong was a third-grade teacher whose classroom was next to Emily's.

"What did you think of the show?" Margie asked.

Emily shook her head and answered, "It seems like a lot of work for a small amount of attention."

Jamison's face livened up, and he exclaimed, "Yes! That's exactly right! I agree with one hundred percent. These companies take advantage of the working-class teacher and convince them that these things will make them better grade-school teachers. They don't, though, and not a lot of people get it."

Emily's eyes were big as she listened to the diatribe that Jamison just went on. *A simple 'I agree' would have been fine.*

"Oh, hush your face, Jamison. You always get yourself worked up," Margie said.

Margie Furlong had been a staple in Marie-Glen Elementary for the past fifteen years. Throughout her tenure, she watched her three children grow up and go to school. In 2010, her son, Ryan, died from atelectasis, a condition where all, or part, of a lung becomes airless and collapses. The grief took its toll the following weeks, and she voluntarily placed herself in psychiatric care for a month. After her visit, she appeared to back to her usual self, but her apathy was apparent; nothing made her excited, at least in a real way. A few years back, Margie's husband died, and even though she still had two of her kids and now grandchildren, she seemed to get worse.

"A word of advice to you, honey, just play along. You'll feel more at home if you can just learn to play the game like me and, once in a blue moon, Jamison."

Jamison raised his coffee in the air, acknowledging what Margie said without averting his eyes from the newspaper he was reading. "Thanks, Margie, and screw you very much!"

"You're welcome, dear, and not even if you let me videotape it," Margie replied.

"Fair enough," Jamison immediately retorted. There was a kind dialogue they had with one another that seemed to Emily like it was going on for years. They were quite different in age, but Jamison came across like an old soul. Margie stopped caring a while back and reverted to a spryer version of herself. Somehow, it worked for them both.

"Is that what you do? Just pretend to care in a stupid popularity game?" Emily asked. Margie stood up to start walking back to her class. She took Emily's arm, and they both started walking out the door into the halls.

"Bye, Jamison," Margie said. Jamison waved his pinky finger as a replacement to a simple goodbye. As they walked, Margie explained, "When it comes down to it, people are people, and all they want is to be heard in the long run. They want inclusion and recognition, whether they know it or not, and that goes for us. For me, I don't really care about items, family photos, or baby pictures. I just go along with it because I know it makes them feel good."

"You don't really care that much," Emily reiterated.

"Oh, no dear. Look at me. I'm dead inside!"

Both laughed as they walked to their classrooms. "I think you are like me in some ways, and I think you need to find out what is important to you. I just know it's not an electronic stapler."

Emily smiled at her school neighbor and proclaimed, "I think you may be my new best friend."

Margie smiled and replied, "I'm not going to go to any of your candle parties or go clubbing so that you know."

"I'd rather rip my fingernails out," Emily said, assuring Margie.

"Good answer, girl. Good answer."

4

"It sounds like you had a little bit of a clique at the very least," Paul assumed.

Emily nodded in agreement as she thought about the good times and the inside jokes she had with Margie and Jamison.

"I can say with some certainty that they helped me get through the days. I loved the kids I taught, but they could drive a sane person to the nearest asylum." After a moment of reflection, Emily decided to talk about her friends a bit more.

"Jamison was a younger, single guy, who was always on the lookout for a potential girlfriend," she began, as Paul cracked a smile. "It got to a point where he was just looking for any female that would give him the time of day. One day, Margie said that he was so horny that if someone threw a roast beef sandwich in the air, he would probably screw it before it hit the ground!" Emily fell forward, laughing as Paul watched her turn red from not being able to catch her breath. A few snorts came out of her, which embarrassed her whenever that happened. Most people found it endearing, but she tried not to laugh too hard, usually because she didn't want others to judge her. Paul was relieved. It was the first moment that pure humanity was finally shining through and not just the shell of a person who walked into his room earlier. At one point, the often talked about but never heard a snort from her laugh was evident to Paul. Emily calmed down because she realized that another person listened to her snort for the first time since Crosby. While it felt good to laugh after the last few weeks, Emily fell back in her slump because she began to think of Crosby.

"Did I do something wrong?" Paul asked.

"No," Emily answered, "Just remembering is all." There was a hint of sadness from her reply that was different from her melancholy from the shooting. Even though Emily said that what happened to her class was her fault because she could have done more, her relationship with Crosby saddened her. It may have been all of her doing.

"I would like to talk about Crosby a bit more, for a second, if you don't care," Paul inquired. Paul wanted to keep the conversation on the light side; he wanted to see her remember the good parts.

Emily nodded in agreement with a stipulation, "Not a lot, though, okay?"

"Why?" he asked Emily.

The truth was that she didn't want to talk about Crosby at all but keeping her "shrink" happy would be an excellent gesture to maybe getting a clean bill of mental health. The truth was that the more Emily told Paul about her love, the sooner the session would end, and she didn't want that for more reasons than one. One of the reasons was having to go back out into the world again, which was the last thing she wanted.

"Because if I tell you everything now, then my story won't flow correctly. Spoilers, my dear head doctor. We don't want that." Emily answered with a hint of flirtation.

"When did you know? When did you know that he was the man you wanted to be with?" Paul bluntly asked.

Emily took a deep breath and answered, "Almost immediately."

Intrigued, Paul sat back, waiting for Emily to tell a story like a child getting ready to sleep, but she didn't and left it a mystery once again.

"If there is anything that most people know about Crosby is that he loves fireworks. He always had a fascination with them; when they went off, he stopped what he was doing to find them and then became entranced with the sky's lights. The first and only time we went overseas was to visit England while still in college. There was a fireworks display during Bonfire Night, and he never looked at the fireworks; he just looked at me. When I asked him why he wasn't watching what he loved, he replied, 'I love you like fireworks.' That was it. I knew he was the one before, but that man forced me to love him more. It was a great night... and a great trip." Emily grinned, knowing what happened later that night. She would have been too embarrassed to confide those intimate details with Paul.

"Tell me about the trip," Paul inquired.

"No," Emily whispered while looking away into the light beaming through the window as she became lost in her memories, "I think I'll keep that one for me."

5

Paul always found it strange how a human's emotions could go from lighthearted and fun, then go to a very dark and depressing place in such a short amount of time. He knew to talk about friends would get Emily out of her head for a few minutes, but inevitably, like most of his people, the melancholy set back in. Paul Cusick typically dealt with mentally broken individuals who suffered a tragic loss or had memories of a happening that didn't go exactly how they remembered, causing them to put added guilt upon themselves, where none was justified. Paul knew the complications of Emily's psyche but attempted to help anyway; it was his job, after all, from the higher-ups that be. Now it was time to go back to work.

"I saw them about a week and a half ago," Emily mumbled.

Paul poked his left ear forward and said, "Come again?"

Emily cleared her throat and repeated what she had said.

Paul was confused. "Do you mean the children?" he asked, "Because we already started talking about that."

Emily rolled her eyes and replied passive-aggressively, "No, Paul! Not the kids, Margie and Jamison." Emily was becoming more hostile. All Paul could do was ask himself if it was talking about her fiancée, Crosby, that set her off or if she was heading towards a breakdown.

"They just popped out of nowhere when I was in town going to the grocery store," Emily said.

"Had you seen them any time before then? Right after the shooting?" Paul asked.

She shook her head as she tried to remember for sure. Everything had happened so fast for her mind to process. The last thing Emily remembered about that day was coming home and the start of the chattering noises entering her consciousness.

6

Where are you going? Remember. You're stuck. I'm stuck. Why can't you see what you need to?

"Jesus!" Emily yelled out loud, waking from another nightmare. Panting heavily, she looked around the room to see if anyone was around her. The notion of someone else being in her home seemed ridiculous. Still, ever since she woke to find deceased children circling the bed and seeing things through her peripheral vision, what she learned in Catholic school made her wonder about the afterlife.

The day she woke up and saw several of the children she taught and grew to love that had died that day a week and a half ago, she couldn't let go of what it all meant. Their gray and black visages haunted her mind. When they ran away from her after Emily began to yell in horror, they left their dark residue on the dark hardwood floor—a mark to remind her that what she saw could be real. The blots of black never disappeared, and no matter how hard she tried, no matter how much she scrubbed or used her nails, Emily could not get the darkness off the floor.

Most of Emily's dreams now were filled with voices muttering sentences that didn't make sense to her. She never believed in signs, but she also wondered if some divine force was trying to veer her toward a specific direction.

The apartment was just as cold and empty as it had been for the last week or so. Emily's typical routine was to wake up, grab a coffee, maybe a muffin, and sit down in front of her laptop to watch online videos. Now she just wakes up from whatever voice-filled nightmare plagued her that night. Even her appetite was cause for concern as she never ate what she made for herself, a glass of milk and a chocolate muffin. *I have the appetite of a three-year-old, apparently.* It was the same breakfast she had the morning of the shooting. As she glared at the food, she realized that she didn't eat the food then either; *have I been subconsciously making the same meal repeatedly?* Emily walked to the window that faced the town square. She looked out among all the people walking to work, cars driving around the roundabout, and kids bouncing around their friends to go to school—all the things ordinary people do. Emily smiled at the people going on with their lives. A man in a blue blazer and plaid button-up shirt stopped and faced her building and looked up to her apartment window. She squinted her eyes to see if it was anyone she knew. The man turned his head to talk to another person, this time a brunette in a black dress with yellow flowers. She conversed with the man and then turned around, looking up in Emily's direction.

What the hell is going on?

Another young woman walked up to the sidewalk from across the street carrying a bouquet. She looked at the other two people and, like them, brought her head up to investigate Emily's home. Then more came; one, two at a time. They stared at Emily in the window, then the children arrived. Not just the regular children who waited along with all the adults that filled the sidewalk onto the street. It was the dark ones. The ones she saw before—her students. They came from all directions, and they took their time walking to the crowd that faced her window.

What is wrong with them? Why do they look so malevolent? What happened to them, and why are they still here? She knew what happened to them, but then it was a cruel mistress that feeds on the innocent if there was an afterlife. As they slowly walked to her building, they began to point their fingers in the air at Emily. A faint sound of moaning became louder as they drew closer, and following them were the adults. Their eyes, filled with blackness, began to leak the substance that surrounded them like they were crying. Pointing and bellowing, the children ran toward Emily's building.

They weren't just adults; they were the parents. Emily could recognize a set of them by their overweight physique. Bo Gentry's parents were evident as they were the last parents she saw before the incident. That and they were fatter than the other parents. The children were attached to their parents in death as they were in life, and while it was sweet in a morbid way, Emily couldn't handle it. She couldn't keep her eyes off them either as seven of the kids in her class came to the building: Jaime Renee Cassidy, Derek Singletary, Bo Gentry, Sloane Chastain, Ava Nauling, Feng Song, and Brad Medler.

Some of them began to slow down while others ran ahead, but everything was happening in slow motion for Emily. As the others reached the sidewalk, poor Ava fell on her knees, coming off the curb. Sweet Ava, she always was clumsy with big pop-bottle glasses. Ava turned over on her rear and reached for her knee to cradle. She melted down and cried, letting out big alligator tears. The darkness that surrounded the children began to stretch toward Ava as she cried. How? I...I...I don't get it!

Are you okay? What happened? Get up; it's just a scratch. You just need to stand up. It's okay, don't cry. Dilly-dally-shil-lyshally. It hurts!

Emily could hear the children speaking to one another. The black substance that wrapped around the children began helping Ava rise, guiding her to her feet. The darkness from the other six had made its way across the concrete. As the sludge crawled further away from their hosts, it started to pull them closer to Ava as if it were a guide for their souls. There was no way to know if the children knew what their spirits were doing for Ava or if she even knew. Still, as she rose to her feet, she looked directly at Emily, yelled, and pointed towards her.

The other kids looked at Ava and followed her finger to where she was pointing. Their black eyes grew big, and as their mouths opened to yell towards Emily, the muck that engulfed them began to pour out of them even more. The children's yells and moans muffled as Emily saw their mouths trying to spout out words. *What are you saying? I don't understand!* The moaning and yelling started to get louder, and as she cupped her hands over her ears, Emily ran towards her front door. *It can't be. This isn't real! No way! Why? I'm sorry! We didn't mean to! You look so sad. Peez, you haft to weev!* It was them. She could recognize those small voices no matter how incoherent the words they spoke were.

The door was difficult to open. It always was. The harder Emily grabbed the knob, the easier her hand slipped off it. After multiple turns of the knob with no success, Emily took a deep breath, put the palm of her hand on the knob, and carefully twisted it. Why was that so damn hard? The wailing of the upset children started to fade, and all Emily could think about was how she needed to know, how she needed them to be okay, and why they couldn't move on. *You're one to talk.*

Emily dashed out of her apartment and made a break for the stairs that led out to the alleyway she and Crosby would use to enter the building. As she ran past her landlord's antique shop, she saw Claire staring outside again. She listened to the radio commercials on the local oldies station.

"We want you to know that you are fine the way you are, but if you need someone to talk to, Dr. Paul Cus..." could be heard before the static of the station set in for a moment. The children's crying began to fade away faster. Emily listened to the ad but didn't pay much attention as she had more pressing matters.

As she walked towards the street outside her building, Emily saw some people looking at her. Instead, they just looked at the facility as Claire seemed to put up a banner for her store, but Emily couldn't see what the sign said. They weren't even looking at me. I am so conceited sometimes; however, that still didn't explain her students appearing from beyond. As she looked down onto the middle of the square, she saw decorations placed on a giant board. "It is getting to be fall soon, and I bet they are putting out the big decorations for the state committee," she thought aloud. After realizing that she was vocalizing her thoughts, Emily put her hand over her mouth to see if anyone noticed; no one did.

The echoes of children yelling and crying were faint. One last yelp from one of the kids brought her attention across the street near the theater. A small black dot disappeared over the horizon as Emily found what she was looking for but was too slow to reach them. *This won't be the last time. I know it.*

She scared them away. They ran as soon as she came down the stairs, which disappointed Emily. Why are they scared of me? I'm supposed to be the one frightened of them. None of this made any sense to her, and she was no better off than she was a couple of weeks ago. It was infuriating because all Emily wanted to do was tell them that she was alright and that they could go on to whatever life was waiting for them.

After gazing upon the town square, Emily realized that it wasn't the fall decorations at all. The volunteers were hanging orange and blue streamers and banners for a fundraiser held for the Marie-Glen Elementary families shooting families that happened a week ago. The signs alone were enough to trigger Emily's flashbacks and post-traumatic stress.

It was October 15th again. "Not again. Not again!" Emily cried. It wasn't like it was before. All the kids were doing an art project, sitting in their seats with their arms folded and feet flat on the floor, which was a surprise—every one of them dressed as if it were picture day at the school.

Emily went into teacher mode automatically without understanding what was going on. She knew she was hallucinating but couldn't help but to play her part in it. "Where were we?" she asked, trying to complete the fantasy.

"We were about to leave Ms. Sinclair," one of her students said.

Confused, Emily asked, "Where were we going to go?"

Derek Singletary raised his hand and replied, "We're going to get our picture taken today. That's why we look so dang good!" The children all smiled at once and laughed at the same time while staring at Emily. There was something wrong with their eyes; they didn't blink.

Suddenly a man with a camera appeared behind Emily. He seemed like a professional photographer with a winning smile. Dressed in a black button-up shirt and jeans, the photographer looked at Emily. As his grin grew wider, he asked, "Is it okay to get started, Ms. Sinclair?"

Emily nodded slowly and looked back at her class.

"Okay, everyone!" she exclaimed, "Let's put on our smiles and all at once say 'cheese!'" As she looked around the room, all her kids were already smiling—so hard it made Emily's face hurt.

"We don't say 'cheese' anymore," Feng Song said.

"Well, what do we say then?" Emily inquired.

Jamie Renee raised her hand. She was so angelic with her big doe eyes. Jamie was always a joy to Emily; she was a handful because of her deafness, but Emily loved it, and she loved it when she was happy.

Emily pointed to Jamie and asked, "Yes?"

Her hand made the form of a gun with her pointer finger pointed at Emily, and her thumb was mimicking the hammer. She brought her thumb down and pulled her hand back like a pistol going off. Jamie then pointed to herself.

"I don't understand," Emily said as she shook her head, but she already knew what she was singing to her, and she hoped it wasn't right.

"Shoot me!" Sloane said. Then all the children started to chime in as they signed and repeated it over again. As it began to turn into a chant, the children's smiles grew fuller to something that didn't resemble humans. Their smiles, from each side of their mouths, reached their ears. Their flesh began to tear from the middle of their faces. The sound of cracking bark and branches echoed in the room. Blood emerged from their split apart faces. Grains of dirt slowly poured from their eyes and ears into their wide-open mouths. The children began to choke on the earth they were now buried under, not appearing human.

The photographer moved his face closer to Emily's and whispered, "Is it okay to start now?"

Emily's voice was no longer her own. She wanted to yell, "No!" and "Get out!" But all that came out of her was a faint whisper, "Yes."

The photographer grinned harder and turned around toward the children seated behind their desks. "Okay, kids," he yelled, "Say 'shoot me!'" They couldn't say anything; they were suffocating, gasping for breath with terrifying smiles that stretched the flesh on their faces past each of their limits. The children stood up and yelled, "Shoot me!"

Emily looked down, and instead of a camera, the man was pointing a shotgun toward her children. The little ones that she was supposed to look after.

"No!" Emily screamed.

The room went dark, and the first shot went off, and it flashed like a camera bulb, making a shattering sound. When the light flashed, Emily saw a glimpse of Bo Gentry in his seat with a shotgun wound to his chest.

Another blast came from his gun. Emily heard glass shattering again, like an old camera used in the mid-twentieth century. As the light flashed, she saw Ava Nauling go from smiling hard for the camera to sitting down with her head lying on her desk. Blood trickled from the fresh hole in her head onto the floor. Each drop of innocent blood echoed through the room.

"Stop!" Emily finally yelled, but the shooting didn't stop.

Emily watched as her students were murdered one by one as their bodies fell into different poses every time a flash of light came from the shotgun. In the end, the children stayed in their seats or were knocked backward from the blast of the weapon. Soon the lights went off for good, and Emily Sinclair collapsed onto her knees and heard the man responsible for the act ask, "Would you like these in gloss or matte?"

7

A bullhorn's sound brought Emily back into reality as a man was signaling were to set a stage up near the gazebo in the town square. The powers that be in Marie-Glen decided that the fundraiser would be in thein the middle of all the small shops circling in the area. She found herself on her knees with her hands clenched together, unwilling to stand back up. Emily wondered if she had recently been so far out of the loop. Could an event such as this have possibly passed without her knowing? If she was anything, Emily always checked the town's website for all local activities and made it a priority to go. Not because she wanted to necessarily, but she liked the idea of being seen and known by others. Crosby didn't have the same sentiment as his fiancée as he found it best to be in the shadows and keep the friends you already have instead of making fake ones.

Clack-clack-clack-clack-clack. That sound was back again, louder than it had ever been before. Emily didn't know where it was coming from but was sure she could find it. Moving her head right to the left, narrowing in on the location, pointing her ears toward the sound, Emily eventually closed her eyes again. She focused her hearing on the terrible noises. *It's coming from the right.*

Bringing her head up, Emily looked to her right side. It was coming from the same direction as the elementary school. There was a wooded area down the street before one would reach the school if they were walking or driving, and in between the trees, nine children stood. They were glowing. *Maybe not glowing.* The children had a white hue about them, which Emily thought she could not see entirely. The ghostly children observed Emily from afar. She didn't recognize them, but most people wouldn't be able to from that far away, to be fair. Still, something was unnerving about them.

"I have been in that apartment too long," Emily said to herself, "I need to get out and go to the store or something." Emily walked back into her apartment to find her purse. After much searching and belting out numerous expletives from frustration, the only thing she could see was her matching wallet that went with it. Emily started to remember that last day, realizing that she brought her purse to school that day but left her bag. She remembered being mad the previous day because she couldn't buy a cup of overpriced coffee.

Walking down the stairs again, Emily investigated the antique shop to find her landlord, Claire, asleep at the cash register. The day for her was coming to an end. *Bless her heart; she's so old. It's probably getting close to bed for her.* The radio was still blaring throughout the shop. Emily took a moment to forget the outside world and found the time to walk into the store and turn down the volume. She debated whether she should wake her, but Claire looked so peaceful and comfortable that Emily didn't have the heart.

Emily crept out of the shop and out the side door. When she walked outside again, she was startled by her friends and peers, Jamison Smith and Margie Furlong. "Jesus!" Emily yelled. She was glad to see her friends again, but it also caused her heart to skip a beat. *I thought it did, at least.* "You scared the shit out of me!" she said as she laughed to herself, but by looking at the faces of her friends, they were in no mood for jokes.

"Did you see her?" Margie asked.

Confused, she looked over to Jamison for some clarification, which he did not give. "Who?"

"Her," Jamison hissed, "Rachael!"

Emily put her finger in the air and retorted, "Watch the tone, dude. I will beat your ass and pray for forgiveness later." Emily then realized who they may have been talking about. "Rachael? McKay?" she asked.

Both nodded in agreement.

Still jumbled, Emily simply asked, "What about her?"

"She is stalking us," Margie answered.

Emily was taken back at the news for a moment. "You mean Ms. One Up?" she asked to make sure everyone was on the same page.

"Yes," Jamison whispered, "She was watching me from across the street!"

Margie nodded her head quickly and added, "She was in my house!"

Emily didn't believe what she was hearing, which was hypocritical due to the strange things she had seen over the week.

Emily started to think back to all the jokes they played on one another over the months and thought she knew what they were up to, and it was disturbing. She smiled and asked, "Are you messing with me? Is this like when Jamison put his cell phone in my classroom with the vibration on high and convinced me that you lost your vibrator and had me try to find it, Margie?"

Margie poked Emily in the breast to bring her back to their level.

"Ow," Emily yelled, "You poked me in the tit!" Emily expected to see them laughing, but they weren't. They were terrified. Margie put her hands-on Emily's shoulders, and as sincere as she had ever seen her friend, Emily shut her mouth and listened.

"She keeps her back to ya," Margie whispered, "She blends in with everyone really well, but if you acknowledge her, she starts to follow you."

Emily bit the bottom of her lip, trying to keep from responding with a negative remark. "And she doesn't stop when you leave the area... she follows you home," she continued. Emily looked at Jamison to verify he had seen it as well.

"What about you?" Emily asked Jamison.

Jamison took a deep breath and looked upwards to collect his thoughts on the matter. "Yes, but not the same way exactly.," he answered as he shifted his eyes from right to left, leaning towards Emily. "Rachael was down the alleyway between the Hawkins Restaurant and the movie theater. She was at the end of it with her back turned from everyone like a dirty, shameful secret. I saw her through the corner of my eyes. When I stopped, I didn't turn my head, but I knew that she did. I could hear the bones in her neck pop as she twisted her head, and her teeth were chattering. When I mustered up the courage to look, she was white. White as our eyes, with blue pupils that could pierce through your soul."

Emily shook her head in disagreement as she may have known something they didn't. "Rachael McKay died a day or two ago. It was all over the local news as the "Teacher Whose Guilt Killed Her.""

She wasn't exaggerating. Poor Rachael McKay, the girl who just wanted to be liked but did so in uncouth ways, was given a title based on the suicide note she left before her landlord found her hung from her ceiling. Her wrists and ankles were sliced all to hell from the repeated attempts to cut her veins open. It just hurt significantly, or so the coroner assumed, so asphyxiation was preferable in comparison. Rachael's suicide note was an overall explanation of her guilt over several of her students shot and killed on her watch. The consistent blame she placed on herself and the overwhelming negativity placed upon her from the community was too much. Not all the children died, but when a person compared the measures other teachers took to ensure safety, one could see it negatively. Emily could understand the feeling. She had been hiding in her empty, drafty apartment for the last week. The burden of thinking that it was her fault that her children died was overbearing. Emily and Rachael failed to understand that the notion of being a protector of others was conceited. It was not their fault. The man with the shotgun on the 15th of October was to blame.

"We know, but you have to admit there is something strange going on—gray children with black eyes that look like smoke. Pale kids with blue eyes as well; we see them in the distance. They were spread out before, but now they seem to be coming together more," Jamison explained, like one of his many other conspiracy theories. Emily couldn't argue as she had seen what he had described.

"What is it? I mean, if you had to take an educated guess, what do you think is going on?"

Margie brought her old, cracked lips toward Emily's ear and whispered, "I don't know if they know they died. If that's not it, I am afraid of what will happen when they get closer to us." Emily's eyes widened, and she immediately confessed, "They were around my bed. The gray children were. They looked like some of my students, and they were in my home. When I woke up, they scurried away like mice."

Margie stepped back from Emily and replied, "I am not so sure it's the grays you need to worry about, dear."

Emily wondered if that was true, then what threat do the others pose to her and her friends? *This is nonsense! They're dead. That's it!*

Margie and Jamison started to step away from Emily. "We have to go now," Margie said as they began to turn their back to her.

"Wait!" Emily demanded, "When will I see you again?"

Jamison and Margie turned around to look at Emily for what they thought could be the last time. "I'm not sure, girl," Margie replied, "I am not sure if we're right for this place anymore."

It took a few moments for Margie's words to sink into Emily's mind, realizing that her friends were going to leave the place that so much horror and drama had resided. Emily's tears started to build in her eyes. "Where will you go?" she asked, holding back from sobbing, holding back the tears.

Jamison turned around and answered, "Not sure, but there are plenty of places that could be better, and it's okay to let go of your past. There are always options; maybe not the ones you want, but they're always there if you are willing to look."

That was the most profound that Jamison Harris—the girl-crazy, conspiracy-theorizing, self-obsessed loner—had ever been. He never said much, but when he did, it was usually worth listening to. Over time the wall that he had put up around himself started to crumble and now may have been the final rock that shattered to make him whole.

Emily waved to her friends as they walked to their homes to try to forget that day and, probably, every day afterward. Both had a point; why stay when there is nothing left? But then there was the adage that her father always said, "*Just because you leave the place doesn't mean it will ever leave you.*" Emily's stubbornness would keep her in Marie-Glen because it was what she wanted. Leaving, in her eyes, would be cowardice.

Margie Furlong and Jamison Harris were gone, and Emily felt alone—truly alone. She knew it was nice for her to have people around if she needed them in the back of her mind, but she never reached out to them. As usual, she shut herself away from those that could and perhaps wanted to help. *Sometimes people become broken and need the extra ear to listen to them. Sometimes people just want to be heard, and sometimes it only takes one to do it.* But that probable "one" was gone due to her inability to understand. Emily knew that now but not when it mattered the most with Crosby.

As Emily composed herself, brushing off any possible tears from her face, she lost the urge to go to the store. She knew that she had to blow the proverbial stink off her and get out more, *but not today.* Emily went back through the door that leads to the staircase to her apartment. Making sure she wouldn't wake Claire from her slumber, Emily walked through the door and lightly closed it behind her. She didn't realize that an entity blended in with the white wall beside her. It was Rachael McKay.

Facing the wall, Rachael slowly looked behind her shoulders to see if Emily would notice; she didn't. Rachael turned her head back around slowly, waiting for the time where Emily would see. What Rachael always wanted was to be seen. *"I left, and it wasn't right. I left, and it wasn't right."* Emily stopped halfway up the staircase, startled by the voice behind her. Scanning the stairs and the walls beside her, Emily couldn't find the person that went with the voice. The person sounded melancholy with some anger mixed in. *I left, and it wasn't right;* that sentence kept lingering in Emily's head.

"Hello?" she nervously said aloud. Emily should have turned around to climb the rest of the stairs that creaked every time she stepped, but something made her look at the bottom of the stairs.

Something was wrong. There was something off about the way the hall looked from her view. *"The walls,"* she thought, *"There was something wrong with the walls."* Specks of black had appeared. Concerned that black mold had begun to manifest, Emily walked down the stairs to inspect the growth that had occurred on her landlord's bottom floor wall. Leering at the black specks, Emily gently rubbed her finger against one of them. A vibrating sensation tickled her right pointer finger, and the bit flew away. It was a fly.

Emily looked at the other specks to verify they indeed were flies as well. They were, but they appeared to be stuck in the wall as if they landed in fresh, white paint, and it had dried around them. There was something not right as Emily began to see hairs caked into the color that was never there before. Emily doubted herself because she never made it a habit to inspect the paint job. It wouldn't have been unheard of with her obsessiveness about minor details. *I'm almost positive this wasn't here. Did Dubois paint the bottom floor recently?*

There was a sense of unease in the air. The ambient sound that could typically be heard from the town outside was muted. Emily could only hear the flapping of insect wings; it was the only thing she could. Reaching for the handrail behind her, Emily climbed the stairs, looking back at the wall every so often. When Emily came to the second floor, she looked down one last time. She wasn't sure why she needed to. *There wasn't really any reason to.*

A piece of the wall moved. The paint, from Emily's perspective, started to inflate, creating a melon-sized bubble. A set of eyelids opened, revealing ice blue pupils in the white protrusion as chips of paint crumbled to the floor. It wasn't a bubble of white color; it was the head of a woman camouflaging her body, revealing herself to Emily. The fly's wings flapped as a pale woman pushed herself out of the wall. Strands of wet, white paint mixed with dark, dead skin attached to Rachael's face slowly drooled onto the floor. The insects tried to fly away, pulling the woman's hair with them but became ensnared in the tangled mess. "I left, and it wasn't right!" she whispered.

Emily fell backward onto the floor. She pushed herself back with her feet to get the woman out of her sight. She didn't want to believe it, but she knew who it was. The stairs began to creak with each footstep the woman took. Rachael was coming for her.

She knew that tiny figure anywhere. Emily didn't have many pleasant feelings about Rachael when they taught together, but she did acknowledge her fit physique. That body was nothing but paleness and rot now as Rachael's body was decomposing. She looked like the children that were getting closer to her, the ones Emily didn't know. "Can you bleed? It looks like you can. I can't." Rachael hauntingly asked as her head emerged into Emily's sight. The rickety stairs creaked louder. The buzzing of flies was the only sound around her as Emily could not hear herself scream anymore.

The walls around her vibrated with every step Rachael took towards her. "Soon," Rachael whispered, "You will start to look like me." She stopped walking, and Emily's will to run had disappeared. Rachael began to laugh as she whispered, "Look at me." The inside of Rachael's mouth was like a dark void as she never closed her mouth. She couldn't close her mouth. There was too much dark ooze circulating in her mouth like death was trying to keep her quiet. *How is she talking to me?* Bringing her fingers to her fly-infested hair, pulling the strands in front of her to view, Rachael began to meltdown. "I'm so ugly! I used to look different. I was pretty, wasn't I?" Emily nodded her head in agreement as she stumbled onto her feet. Inching her way towards her front door, Emily continued to listen to Rachael as she threatened her. "It's too late for me. It's so hot. I know what will happen to me," she began as she began to hiss, "I'm *losing me! They make me! I'm losing myself! I'm sorry! I left, and it wasn't right! They're making me get you! Stay away! I can't help it! They want you! Keep going! Stay away from me! They want me to take you with me!"*

Emily stared at her former colleague. *What had become of her? Why was this happening? Is this what happens when you die?* No, it's what happened to Rachael when she died from suicide. Rachael reached out to Emily, but she didn't want comfort from her. Something was forcing Rachael to want to claw Emily's face off.

The pale corpse's fingers rotted as the skin fell off Rachael's hands with each step. Emily, too shocked to even fathom letting the air release from her throat to scream, began to turn the doorknob to her apartment, but it wasn't angling for her. Every time she reached behind her back to grab the knob, Emily's hand slipped past it, or fate didn't want her to escape. She stopped for a moment, lingering with the thought of leaving this world by the hands of a dead colleague. Like she had before in her dreams when she suffocated in the dirt. *It could be so easy.* The smell of Rachael's putrid breath woke Emily from her daze. She quickly opened the door behind her and walked through the threshold, slamming the door in the apparition's rotted face.

Emily backed herself against the door and slid downward. The familiar sounds of the world around her had slowly started returning. *This is going to get worse before it gets any better.* Her friends were right about Rachael; she was stalking them.

For Rachael McKay, she never had the opportunity to tell her side of the story, not the correct version. She told the police that she could not react to the man entering her classroom that day. "I just reacted without looking at the man and protected the children that I could," was the official statement she gave, but it wasn't the truth. Rachael wasn't in her classroom when the shooter appeared in her class that day. She had an important date with the toilet and her pointer finger going down her throat as her bulimia came into play. Rachael was finishing forcing herself to vomit up her morning cinnamon roll and coffee when the faculty heard shotgun blasts. She liked it when it had enough sugar in the mug that the spoon could stand up on its own. When the sound of gunfire became faint, Rachael ran back to her classroom to find two of her students slumped over; one boy over his desk and another, a girl, off to the chair's side. Spots of blood covered the desks and chairs as the rest splattered onto the floor. The rest of the students had cowered into the corner of the classroom, trembling, and waiting for help. When Rachael came to comfort the rest, all she could feel was shaking, and all she could hear were the judgmental whines; "where were you?" and "aren't you supposed to stay here with us?"

In the end, the word of her abandonment for those few moments circulated through town like a disease. The township and people began to ignore her. As the end drew near, all she wanted to be was someone to say something, yell at her, and make her feel acknowledged. If someone would have told her that it would be okay, or maybe even calling her a fucking twat, anything to make her feel more human and less of a monster. That is what she felt like, a beast. When she died, she created the noose with a belt she put around her neck that did the job. She had attempted to slice her wrists first but found that she couldn't bear the pain of digging sharp, titanium scissors deep into herself. Rachael tried the right wrist first but stopped as the pain was too much for her. She then switched to the left and had more luck, but not enough to finish the job. She was cutting too slow; a fast, deep slice would have been more effective.

For whatever reason, Rachael's tattered body lingered around town to find Emily and the rest of the teachers of Marie-Glen. Emily had only talked to Jamison and Margie about it because they happened to see her exiting the shop, luckily. Like Rachael, she was paranoid about the outside world. She forgot about reaching out to the people she knew best for any kind of guidance. Now the ones that have passed on are the ones looking for her now.

AISLE 10

"What do you think was your best accomplishment in the classroom when you taught?" Paul asked.

Emily took a deep breath and contemplated his question only to let out puffs of air as she exhaled. After looking back over the year and a half of teaching the same kids, there was only one thing that she could think of: how kids, no matter how different they appear to be, can be empathetic to one another.

"I would have to say pairing them up in their seating arrangements," she finally answered.

Paul looked confused and asked, "Normally, I would expect to hear about improving grades or speech. How did the seating assignments help?"

Without hesitation, Emily answered, "Because when you stick two people together that seemingly have nothing in common, sometimes you get to see what being human is all about.

2

It was getting close to Marie-Glen Elementary winter break, and the children were becoming antsy. With only a couple of days left, all the teachers took the opportunity to make the classroom a fun environment. That and they had nothing left in the curriculum to teach for the semester.

Emily took the time and opportunity to teach the class about the holidays from other religions. At this point, the kids clung to every word that Emily Sinclair said. She had gotten through to them in a way that no other teacher could, and the faculty knew it.

"What is the sign for giving, or to give?" Emily blurted to make sure the children were on their toes.

Without hesitation, they held their thumbs to their fingers on their dominant hand and moved them away from their bodies. The motion looked like you are giving the other person something.

Emily nodded in agreement and let the kids work on their arts and crafts. They cut red, green, and white construction paper to make loops and interchange them to decorate the room with streamers.

"Mr. Song!" Emily blurted.

Feng rose to his feet as he tended to when called upon and answered, "Hai! I mean, yes."

Emily chuckled and asked Feng to tell the class how to say 'Give' in Japanese, please.

"Ataeru," he told the class.

"Can you repeat that, everyone?" she asked, but she demanded it. The class repeated. Jamie Renee was confused, looking around, wondering what just happened. For once, Emily was oblivious to her frustration. Jamie sighed and went back to the art project, determined to say something to Emily about it.

Emily sat down at her desk and watched her class and how everyone appeared to be content. Sloane Chastain and Ava Nauling were about as opposite as it got. One from an over-privileged lineage of wealth and the other with almost nothing to her name. Over the last few months, Ava has helped Sloane and her reading because of her dyslexia problem. At first, Sloane was repulsed at the idea of someone like Ava helping her as if she were a beggar on a street corner, but something changed over the weeks. Sloane went from complaining about the way Ava smelled, sitting next to her, to having more compassion. It isn't easy for many to admit when they need help, and Sloane never did. Ava just offered it without any notion of wanting something in return. *Something for nothing.* It was a concept that confused Sloane.

Sloane wore a charm bracelet that clanged together whenever she moved her right hand. Ava was always mesmerized by her bracelet. For the last several weeks, she asked Sloane if she could 'jingle her jangles.' Being who she was, Sloane was very hesitant of anyone coming close to touching her, but she grew used to it over time.

On this day, Emily witnessed humanity at its best. Sloane put down the construction paper and started to reach for her book bag. She wanted to wait until the last day, but she was too excited to wait.

"I have something for you," Sloane said as she bent over to look in her bag. Ava pushed her glasses closer to her face, wondering if she heard Sloane correctly. The phrase "I have something for you" was not heard that often in Ava's life, so she was intrigued at what Sloane meant.

Sloane gently pulled out a silver bracelet and showed it to Ava.

"It's so pretty," Ava said with her eyes big through her glasses, "You're so lucky!" Sloane grinned and started to put it on Ava's right wrist. "It's not mine, weirdo. It's yours!"

Ava's mouth swung open and staying ajar that way as Sloane placed it onto her wrist. Twirling the bracelet around her wrist, Ava heard a jingle. She turned the bracelet around to find a charm in the shape of a pair of glasses. "Oh," she exclaimed, "Because I wear glasses!"

Sloane grinned and nodded her head.

Ava bounced up and down in her chair and yelled, "Thank you!" as the rest of the class took notice. She put her arms out to hug Sloane.

Sloane started to back away, thinking that they weren't at that point in their friendship to be doing that until she thought about 'giving.' Sloane gave in a little. She put her arm around her as Ava went all the way with the hug. It went on for a few moments until Sloane eventually said, "Okay. I think we're good now."

Emily laughed a little. Not at Sloane being uncomfortable, but at the kindness that she was able to muster. *Will wonders never cease? These small hearts are good.*

After a few relaxing moments, the classroom intercom sounded with Dean Williams, the principal, at the other end. *"Ms. Sinclair,"* he said, *"Could you please come to my office when you get a moment?"*

Emily rolled her eyes and agreed.

"Well, class, it appears like your teacher may be in trouble," she exclaimed.

The kids laughed and replied with an "Oooohhhhhh!"

Emily put her hands up and said, "All right, settle down." Walking over to the door that led to Margie Furlong's class, she caught sight of Jaime Renee, giving her what she could only describe as 'the stink eye.'

Swinging the door open, Emily asked Margie to keep an eye out while she went to see Williams. Margie agreed like always when Emily asked her for a favor. "Okay, kids, be good. I will be right back."

Brad Medler, like clockwork, had the response of, "We make no guarantees."

Emily looked back at him and said, "I expect nothing more from you, Mr. Medler."

3

In typical fashion, Emily walked into Dean Williams's office, expecting to butt heads over policy or curriculum. It was automatic that Emily would put up her defenses and ready the sarcasm. She wasn't sure why she was annoyed by him as Williams was simply doing his job. *This is the last guy I need to make an enemy out of.*

They both sat in the office, looking each other up and down. "Did you get the flowers for the holidays?" Dean asked.

Every year the school gives out something to the teachers for the holidays. One year was a mug that said, "World's Best Teacher," but it went to everyone, so it didn't carry any weight. Last year, a box of pens had the school's name on them, and this year was flowers.

"I did get them," Emily answered.

Dean leaned back in his seat confidently and proclaimed, "Those were my idea."

As she was known to do, Emily wanted to roll her eyes to knock down his inflated ego. Instead, she replied, "Well, in that case, I'll make sure they go in some rubbing alcohol." *Even better.*

Dean smirked and sat up in his chair. They were both staring one another down, and as much as they would never admit it, they were more alike than they realized.

"What is it about me that makes you so hostile toward me?" Dean said, breaking his gaze. Emily thought about it for a moment and answered, "I'm not sure. At first, it was just something about your face, and then I figured out that you are extremely arrogant."

Dean scoffed at the notion.

"Look," Emily began, "You have a job to do here, and it cannot be the easiest way to make a living. You have to make sure the curriculum is taught, you know, protocol. Any ideas outside the box are shunned away and are viewed as a waste of time and sometimes obnoxious."

Dean Williams was perturbed at the accusations but was also impressed by Emily's candor. He picked up a file from his desk and decided to get to the business at hand.

"When I heard about you using a noise-canceling headset to teach students what it's like not to hear. I thought it was a little cruel, but the kids seemed to make a little game of it," Dean explained.

Emily began to defend herself, "It wasn't meant to be a game. I was trying to make a—"

Dean interrupted her. "I know what you were trying to do. You decided to teach a foreign language that even some colleges don't offer. Something that is not taught until at least high school for kids...and behind the board's back no less." *Uh oh. This is the part where I lose my job.*

There was a moment of silence as Dean Williams sat back in his chair and announced, "The school board has decided to keep you on, Mrs. Sinclair."

That was unexpected. Emily's demeanor would suggest that she was calm, but she was a little girl giddy over their favorite boy band on the inside.

"Next year, you will teach the fourth grade."

Emily nodded her head and simply replied, "Okay."

Smugly, Dean sat back in the chair and added, "With the same students."

It took Emily a moment to understand what Dean was telling her. Typically, a grade school teacher would have been assigned a new set of students; this was out of the ordinary. "You mean...all the same kids I'm teaching now?"

"Yes, Ms. Sinclair. The same students....and maybe some new ones." Emily sat forward in the old, rusted chair and rested her arm on it. Placing her cheek in her hand, she muttered, "I guess that's okay."

With a devilish smile, Dean responded with a back-handed compliment, "Congrats! You did so well with a group of tough kids that you are now stuck in the same position for another year. How's that for irony?" *English was never my best subject, but I'm willing to bet it isn't irony in the way he thinks. That's more of a win than anything.*

Emily got up from her seat reluctantly and thanked him for letting her stay for another year.

"You know, Ms. Sinclair," Dean said before leaving his office, "Things would be a lot easier for you if you just learned how to play the game. There's nothing wrong with that." Dean was referring to the constant clashing of egos he and Emily were continually having. "Don't aid in ruining a good thing by being you." The southern fire was coming to a head for Emily after that comment.

"No, it would actually be easier on you. Nothing worth having is ever supposed to be easy," Emily explained. She attempted to knock Dean off his proverbial high horse. She shut the door behind her and slowly walked back to class as she strutted down the hall, pleased with herself. Emily wasn't sure what to think of having the same children again for another year; the first had already been so rough. As she walked, Emily thought for sure that the class would be acting up: yelling, throwing supplies, etc. Kids never ceased to amaze the most cynical adults. Emily investigated her classroom through the small rectangular window with the door. She saw that her kids were doing exactly what they should have been doing, creating crafts. *Maybe it won't be so bad after all.*

When the final bell rang, and all the kids rushed out of the class to go home for the day, Jamie Renee slowly got ready. Emily had noticed the frown she wore on her face most of the day. As Jamie approached her, Emily signed, "What's wrong?"

Jamie stopped and looked away as she took a deep breath, with her black hair disheveled as it usually was at the end of the day, mostly from playing with it. Jamie Renee spoke the most words she ever had in front of Emily.

"You umble wen (when) you speak. I can't ep (keep) up!" Jamie said as tears formed in her eyes.

Emily wasn't surprised by how Jamie felt. Since she was a child, Emily tended to mumble a lot; it mostly happened when trying to avoid a conversation. "Umtimes you go from one ubject to nother and I am not ure whad you are alking about." The tears sluggishly trickled from her eyes to her pale skin.

Emily felt horrible at not realizing that she forgot and how easy it was to forget that not everyone hears the same way. She reached out for Jamie's hand and held it; her hand was cold and clammy. "I'm sorry," Emily mouthed slowly to Jamie, "I'll do better. I promise."

Jamie wiped her tears from her face and nodded before she tugged her hand away from Emily and walked out the door to go home. Emily watched as she left and thought about how precious and fragile angels need special handling.

4

"It's good to remember those good pieces of time when you realize something matters," Paul wisely said.

Emily started fidgeting her fingers and biting her nails. She used to have a terrible habit when she was in college before she met Crosby, and it took much hand-slapping from him to get her to quit. Crosby wasn't there anymore, and there was no sign of him. For the last couple of weeks, Emily watched the town square to see if he showed up coming out of one of the shops or just walking around the area.

"Someone told me that you measure your life by the moments you remember most because that is all life is: a series of moments that shape you into the person you are," Emily quoted, "But when I think of all my moments, I can't think of any of the good ones. Does that mean I had a bad life?"

Paul shook his head and replied as he pondered, "That's just the human mind; we look at all the great things in our past when our present is good. It's when it's bad that the darkness overtakes it."

Both fell silent as they reflected on their words. "Not that it makes a difference, but I think that you have way more good things than bad or melancholy ones," Paul added.

Emily gave a slight smile and replied, "Thanks."

Paul grinned at the notion that something he said may have stuck with Emily. Excited, Paul scoffed and threw his hands in the air; he suddenly realized he wanted to ask about the girls. "What about the two you were just talking about? That's a bond that couldn't be forgotten no matter how hard they tried. That's not nothing, Emily!"

Emily looked away as she knew Paul was right but didn't want to admit it herself.

"Let the sadness go. There is something more for you."

Emily swung her head around to find where the voice came from. There was no one else in the room with them. *Fantastic, now there is a disembodied voice talking to me.* She was sure it wasn't Paul's, but she knew what she heard. It was a woman's voice: a light whisper right into her ear and something not of this world, yet something familiar. The voice echo still resonated in her mind, but it was the sound of the clacking teeth and jaws that interrupted it. Pale children with blue eyes and spine-chilling grins started to put their fingers under the door, trying to pull it open. The blackness of their decaying nails rubbed off onto the grooves of the hardwood floor. So many tiny, ghostly fingers were shoved under the door that the sound of small bones snapping in half curdled Emily's blood.

I wanna see it! Shut up! There will be a time and place, they said. It's taking too long. Why do we look like this?

Emily could hear the voices of the children she never knew before the shooting. Were they arguing? Whining? Did they always have a voice?

"You okay?" Paul asked her. As a psychiatrist, he knew she wasn't, but there was always something new going on with her, and he could usually just sense it.

"Yeah," she hesitantly answered, "I thought I heard something." Emily sighed and continued the conversation. "You're right. That was one good thing."

5

It was time to go to the grocery store even though Emily wasn't hungry at all. She didn't have to go as there was enough food in the refrigerator; it was mostly finger foods, but food, nonetheless. It was just a habit for her to go every Wednesday, even though the act of it tested her patience.

She walked into Myer's Grocery that evening, not even knowing what she wanted. Emily crossed the threshold of automatic doors that didn't open for her immediately this time around. It wasn't until another person approached the door that made them open. *Today is just not the day for me to try to be in a good place.*

Gazing upon the aisles, she decided that she didn't need a shopping cart or a basket this time around because Emily wasn't buying much anyway. After identifying the aisles by the signs that hung above them, Emily proceeded to pick up what any newly single woman would want to shove in her mouth, the frozen food aisle. Aisle ten, to be exact.

As she wandered to the back of the store, passing by residents that looked at her like she didn't exist or shouldn't. Emily heard kids laughing on the other side of the store. It started at aisle five, where the condiments were that Emily saw dark shadows using her peripheral vision. It was one of them. *It had to be.* One of her students, shrouded with the darkness that she was used to, was inside the store with her. She knew that laugh: the sound of rich people when they are condescending towards others but with a sweetness to it.

Emily reached the eighth aisle: bread and other carbs. There was another laugh ahead of her, one with a slight snort involved. Looking down the bread aisle, she looked to the right then and left to see the other end. Emily had always seen them one at a time typically. She didn't want to know if there was a second; her curiosity got the better of her.

Emily could hear their whispers echo in her mind. *It's her. What does she want? I don't understand. Does she see us? This isn't her problem anymore. Are we wrong for her?*

She looked down at the other end of the next aisle and looked to both sides. It was empty; conveniently, no one was shopping for bread. The voices had ceased, and Emily let out a sigh of relief.

"Hi, Ms. Sinclair!"

Emily whipped her head back to look down the aisle and saw two dark heads peeking from both sides of the aisle: one with large white eyes and the other squinting. Their voices sounded like an old recording that had been slowed down by pulling on the tape of an old cassette. Both the figures pulled their heads back immediately as if they were playing hide and seek. Shaken, Emily nervously looked ahead and continued to walk to the frozen food area.

This is getting too real. They never talked like that before.

Incessantly looking behind her, Emily began to walk faster to the end of the store, hoping that the two dark entities that were once her pupils would not follow her. At the refrigerated section's cheese portion, Emily looked once more behind her and to her right. There were two women bent over the frozen sections picking out hamburger meat and frozen meals, but that was all. No children.

The music playing in the grocery store blared instrumental versions of the greatest hits from the 80's most of the time while mixing it up with some yacht rock with a few random commercials scattered throughout. *"Are you having a bad day or even a bad month? Just know that you are not alone. Dr. Cusick has helped many sad souls over the years, and he wants to help you..."* followed by the garbled sound of static.

Gliding her hand across the edge of the open freezers as she used to when she was a child, Emily found her way to the end of the aisle. She suddenly stopped with her hand, weighing against the cooler. She leaned her body to see around the corner; *I hope to God that they will not wait for me.* No ghosts were awaiting her arrival.

Emily heard a crumpling sound as she looked down at the cooler next to her. Watching the bags of peas and other vegetable assortments shift around, Emily's mouth began to quiver as she slowly backed away.

"Aren't you cold?" a voice from below the bags asked. A wrinkled gray hand emerged from the cooler and grabbed Emily's; it was freezing as its veins were blue and pulsating. *"I am."*

The bags of food shifted to make way for a glob of hair to emerge out of the cooler. Frozen blonde strands of hair emerged.

Emily knew that hair and forehead from anywhere; it was Rachael McKay. *They were right. Margie and Jamison were right!*

Emily pulled her hand away from the deceased body of Rachael McKay and started to run toward the other end of the store. *Not again!* Turning a Rounding the corner of aisle ten, Emily stopped in front of two girls shrouded in darkness as the rest had been. She stopped in her tracks and looked into each of their eyes; one set grey and the other, white, more significant than the other, like before; they were Ava Nauling and Sloane Chastain. *They must be.* The apparition of Ava was so apparent; her big eyes were from her thick glasses. That's how Emily remembered her eyes being. Sloane's were tiny and judgmental as she typically was in life.

"Why do you hide?" Ava asked in a sweet, deep voice.

Emily shook her head, wanting to explain. "

"Do you not like us anymore?" Sloane continued, speaking in a distorted tone, like someone slowing down a cassette tape.

No. It's not that! I just don't understand. That is what she wanted to tell them, but the words wouldn't come out. Emily couldn't catch her breath as her chest began to hurt, not because of lack of oxygen, but because it felt like someone was ripping her apart.

"Why are you scared of us? Don't you remember?"

Emily put her hands over her eyes, hoping that they would disappear. How would it look to others if she were talking to the air?

Footsteps crept up slowly behind Emily, releasing chunks of ice that fell from its feet. Rachael McKay's rotting corpse was walking toward Emily as frost fell from her tattered, dirty clothes. *Her clothes were so white before. What is happening to her?*

As Rachael moved, her bones crackled, and joints popped out of place. Her head moved abnormally from the bones that broke in her neck when she hung herself with a belt and wrists slashed from the titanium scissors she once coveted.

Emily slowly turned her head to find Rachael's head falling off to the left.

"I'm so cold! Why is it so cold? Why can't I bleed anymore?" She was in agony, and there was nothing Emily or anyone else could do about it. Rachael threw the right side of herself backward to shift her head back onto her neck. Her clothes were covered in ice and dirt; a white, now yellow blouse was torn open, revealing her breasts, and her black skirt split up the side, exposing her legs that were now blue from the lack of blood in her body.

"What is that? What the hell is that?" Sloane deeply whimpered.

Rachael's disincorporated body fell to the ground, and she continued to use her arms to pull herself forward. *"I need your body! I need to feel something. I need to feel you inside me!"* Rachael wanted to make physical contact, but Emily didn't know that she would be taken and consumed for her warmth if she allowed Rachael to grasp onto her. Rachael's rotting corpse wanted to feel something warm, perhaps, but only for a moment.

As Rachael's cold, decrepit arms reached out toward Emily, the girls began to scream. Light emerged from their mouths as they cried out; they were scared for their teacher and themselves. The shrieks and bright lights started to burn the outside of Rachael's dead torso. Backing away from the girls, Rachael yelled and got down on her hands and knees, quickly scuttling away. When she disappeared, Ava and Sloane closed their mouths and started to sniffle. For a moment, the darkness began to dissipate around them to reveal their original forms, the bodies of two girls that Emily once knew. They began to breathe hard and worryingly, as they did not understand what had just happened.

Emily looked at them and watched them begin to break down.

"It's okay," Emily said, attempting to comfort them, "She's gone."

Her words did not comfort them as they began to wail in sadness. As they cried for their teacher, the rest of the patrons inside Myer's Grocery started to stare at them and then toward Emily's direction. They both pointed to Emily as their cries became deafening. Emily placed her hands over her ears and yelled, "Stop it! I don't know how to help you! Tell me what to do!"

Emily thought their souls were in trouble, and it was up to her to figure out a way to save them, but rationally she knew she couldn't, and that broke her heart even more. Emily looked around the store and witnessed everyone around them judgmentally watching as they said, *"What's wrong with you? Don't you know better than to be like this in public?"*

"I'm sorry," Emily said, not knowing what there was to be sorry for as she dashed away from the crowd and out of the store into a town that no longer wanted her.

Sweet Nothings

Not all of Emily's time after the shooting, and until she met with Paul, was all nightmares and dismay; there was enough to reflect on in the past that was good. But the more she thought about Crosby, the more sadness filled her. People like to play therapists and tell each other that they should focus on the good things about people after leaving us in one way or another. Emily was not finding that to be the case.

As Emily played back memories of both her and Crosby in her, she always went back to the same memory, the antique store. She didn't want to think about it, but because of Paul's incessant need to find out why he was no longer around. One that made her smile in such terrible and trying times.

It was close to Marie Glen's town square event to raise money for the victims' families. Emily was sleeping longer each day that went by, and every day with the same dream of facing herself, it was so easy to get lost in it. The notion of sinking into the ground into another plane of existence where no one would ever bother you again wasn't unappealing. Not being able to see the entities haunting you seemed like a sweet escape. However, there was a loving memory that Emily kept clinging to as best she could. It was fading away from her memory. *Not this one. Please not this one.* We all attach to something real when everything else seems to disappear.

2

"Shhhh," Emily emoted to Crosby, "We have to be quiet!"

Crosby knelt in front of the back door to Claire Dubois's antique shop located directly below their apartment. With a hairpin, he tried to unlock the entrance to the shop. In a night of drunken stupor, both Emily and Crosby thought it would be fun to break into their landlord's business. "Why?" he asked.

"Claire is out of town visiting her grandchildren. We have the whole building to ourselves!" Emily started cackling continuously; she was a goofy drunk.

It was the first time either of them had ever really been inside Claire's shop. When Crosby finally picked the lock, the smell of mothballs was imminent. Still, the collection of old items that were once someone's treasure was immense. Claire had typical antique furniture, but more than that, she had old clothing and other various objects scattered throughout. Emily got overly excited by the giant summer hats that wealthy homemakers wore from the 1940s. She frolicked like she was known to do when inebriated. She started to put on the cap and other various, gaudy-looking jewelry from around the store.

As she was playing dress-up, Crosby came across an old top hat and monocle. Emily turned around in her new getup and, mimicking a southern belle, said, "Oh! I do declare, good sir!"

Crosby turned to look at her with the over-sized hat and jewelry and decided to flub a famous line. "Frankly, my dear, I don't give a crap."

Emily giggled and began to rummage through all the other stuff. Emily's getup made Crosby feel a bit aroused.

"Check it out!" Crosby said, excited to show Emily.

As she turned around, she found Crosby dressed like an aristocrat, except her mind went in a more pop culture direction. "You look like the Monopoly guy!"

Crosby then did his rich snob impression, "Mmmm, yes. I just have oodles and oodles of money. Don't I, mumsy?"

Emily suddenly wasn't feeling as silly as she did before as a feeling of desire came over her.

She leaned her body against an old study table meant to house a typewriter and spread her legs a bit. "Just think, Mr. Moneybags, every time you pass go, you collect two hundred dollars from me," Emily said in a playful, seductive tone.

Crosby knew that voice, the "come hither" sound. "Well, I just went past it, and I don't have my money in my pockets," he replied as he walked closer to her.

"Gee, mister.... I don't have that kind of cash on me right now, but maybe I can find something in your pockets?" she playfully explained. Emily licked her lips, waiting for the kiss she knew would come. As Crosby came closer to her from across the room, he saw an old phonograph near the front window. He stopped to put the needle on the record and turned the crank to play what was already on the spinner inside; that was a collection of orchestral ballroom music. The streetlights illuminated the inside of the store just enough to see his love. Still, there was a mystery about what she was doing. The light ran up the left side, and Crosby saw that she had slid up one side of her dress to the top of her thighs. The orchestral violins started to play at the right moment when the role-play was heating up.

"Then I suppose we need to find another form of payment, Ms. Sinclair," he insinuated. He could see Emily's grin on one side of her face, thanks to the street streetlamps.

"But mister, I just moved here from a small town, and I don't know any better. What could I possibly have that you would want?"

Crosby put his hand on her leg and slid it up her thigh. "I'm sure I can think of something, and then we can reach an agreement." They began to kiss passionately and eventually made it to the hardwood floor, where they made love inside Claire Dubois's shop for close to thirty minutes.

Lying on an old quilt on the floor of the shop, Crosby and Emily talked for hours. "Do you think anyone else is doing this?" Emily asked.

Crosby thought for a moment and replied, "What? Breaking into their landlord's shop and doing it on the floor? God, I hope so!"

Emily laughed and slapped Crosby on the shoulder. "I'm serious!"

Crosby was always one to think before he spoke so that what he said would come out as articulate as possible. "My concern would be why wouldn't other people be? To think about people couples who never have, or at least just stopped occasionally to live in the moment like this with their significant others, is kind of depressing." Emily was satisfied with his answer like she typically was and nestled up against his chest.

"Why me?" Emily asked.

"What do you mean?" Crosby replied. He knew what she meant, but Crosby wanted to hear the elaboration.

"You know what I mean. Don't play that game with me."

Crosby laughed because he knew he got caught. "Like that, for example. You call me out on my bullshit, both good and bad. You keep me on my toes."

Emily was not at all satisfied with his answer. "Do better."

Crosby should have known that his answer was not going to be enough. After careful thought, he simply told her the truth: "When I'm with you, I feel whole. I think that you make me a better person or want to be one. You speak your mind when necessary, and even when it's not, you have a way to be sympathetic about it. Whatever I need, you go out of your way to make it happen even though I never ask you. Your skin is smooth, your lips are soft, and when I kiss you and it's like a bolt of lightning goes through me, and I can get through the day better. You are the best part of my life, and I don't know what I would do without you here."

Emily's eyes began to fill with tears of happiness. As sweet as Crosby was to her, she had never heard words like that come out of his mouth. She put her arm around his body and refrained from anything because his embrace was enough.

Crosby chuckled and continued, "But if anyone asks, it's pretty much that I love your ass." Emily pinched his ribs, and they both laughed before Crosby pulled her face toward his to kiss her.

It was that moment in time that Emily clung to the most. There were others but, unbeknownst to her, the memories were fading the longer she stayed in that old apartment. She would never forget Crosby, but holding on to what reminds a person why they attached themselves to another can easily be erased by time without them.

3

"Knock, knock," said a woman's voice said from outside Emily's apartment door. It was the day before she met with Paul Cusick. The inflection of the sound, that of a soft-spoken southern woman, immediately made it clear that her landlord, Claire Dubois, was outside her door. Claire never came to visit that often except for the time when Emily forgot to pay the rent. Emily liked Claire. She was a sweet old woman but had the mouth of a sailor. Emily enjoyed a divine curse word. She typically refrained from saying them because of her job with children, not that it probably mattered because she had heard them blurt out some. *"Lead by example,"* they say. *Boring.*

Emily stumbled off the couch and barely landed on her feet; she felt drunk. *Too much sleep, perhaps?* Dragging her feet to the door, she thought she did something wrong or that Claire would evict her. She looked through the front door's peephole and didn't see anyone standing in front of it.

She slowly opened the door, wondering if someone was playing a prank on her. It wouldn't have surprised Emily if someone had; *this whole town is out to get me.*

Emily slowly poked her head out and looked to her right and saw Mrs. Dubois smiling at her.

"Hello, dearie. I just wanted…Jesus…you like a scared cat in a room full of rocking chairs."

Emily realized that she probably didn't look her best, and her paranoia was showing. *Not one to mince words, I see.*

"Hi, Claire," she said in a bleary voice and a forced smile, "What can I do for you?"

Claire smiled and replied, "Oh, nothing, dearie. I will be away for a while, and I just wanted to see you before I left."

Emily smiled and said, "That means a lot to me. You have no idea."

Claire put her hands up to touch Emily's face as her bottom lip quivered in sadness as she resisted the urge to cry.

"It's okay, dearie," she said in a soothing voice.

Emily wiped her eyes and said, "I know that deep down, but it's just so damn hard to think it."

There was a moment of silence between them both before Claire spoke again.

"You don't have to stay here, you know?" Claire said in a mysterious tone.

Emily looked into Claire's eyes and asked, "What do you mean?"

"Just what I said," Claire clarified, "This place…this town… is nothing but bad memories, and it's okay to get away from all the badness."

Emily started to think about the lease agreement she had with Claire and hurried to remind her of it.

"Oh, pish-posh," she said, "That doesn't matter anymore. It's just a piece of paper, and I highly doubt I will come after you for it."

Emily nodded her head and started to think about her offer to get out of the old apartment. If it weren't for the incident, Crosby would still not be there with her anymore, which would push her towards leaving.

"There is a better place for you now. You just have to put it upon yourself to find it," Claire explained.

Emily's bottom lip quivered because deep down, she knew what was happening. "I'm not sure I know how," she explained as she wiped her eyes.

Claire smiled and replied, "I think you do, and sometimes you have to give in to the signs that are put in front of you."

Emily agreed and asked, "Do you have to go now?"

Claire nodded and started to walk down the hall to the stairs, and before she took a step down, she turned to Emily and said, "Don't worry your head about me, dear; I'm all right." Claire continued to the stairs, but instead of stepping down, she continued to walk ahead, floating in the air and finally disappearing. Emily confirmed what she was afraid of as she fell to her knees and cried for Claire Dubois.

Mrs. Claire Dubois, the owner of Dubois Antiques, died behind the counter of her favorite place to be her antique store. It wasn't much, but it was enough for Claire and a staple in the community. Emily admired that about her—how the most straightforward thing was enough for her in her life. Emily wasn't sad that she died. She simply felt guilty for not realizing Claire had passed when she saw her "asleep" the day before.

Emily walked into her living room, where the sunlight beamed through her large window, illuminating parts of her home. It reminded her of what she always felt heaven would be like: rays of light sporadically cast to brighten portions of the sky that everyone should see. Emily knew Claire had lived a full life and should have been happy that she had moved on, but the reality came to her that she was alone. Her friends moved on to other places, her landlord that she conversed with frequently was gone, and her love, Crosby, had left her.

Emily collapsed onto the hardwood floor and began to sob, which was a common occurrence now. With her head in her hands and tears falling into her palms, she knew that it was time to talk with someone. If Emily didn't leave her apartment and get help soon, one day, she would fall asleep and not wake up from her frequent dream of sinking into the soil, the place where she felt most peaceful.

<u>Boys</u>

"I think we are almost to the end of this session," Paul pointed out. The days were becoming shorter because of the colder seasons approaching. All Emily could think about was what was waiting for her outside the office door. If she were losing her mind, nothing would happen except for the deceased white and dark children of Marie-Glen continuing to appear and drive her further into insanity. If not, she imagined those little hands would grab hold of her and rip her apart until nothing was left.

Emily looked around the room to delay the inevitable. She hoped that Paul wouldn't return to the subject that she had been avoiding all day, Crosby Fulton. Emily's fiancé had suddenly disappeared from her life.

With no context on the reason behind his "vanishing," Paul became impatient with Emily's runaround about the subject. "You know what it's time for," he continued.

Shit. "I can't," Emily whispered.

Paul threw off his glasses onto the table next to him and huffed, "Why!"

Emily turned her head toward Paul as she scoffed at the audacity of Paul, impatient towards her. "What's your problem?"

Paul put his pointer and middle fingers to his temple and started rubbing it. "The problem, Emily, is that you are avoiding what we both know is a major turn in your life. I need to know what's going on in there before the day is out. That is all the time that they are giving me!"

Who is? The school board? The county?

Sticking her neck toward him, like a snake about to feast, Emily put her finger in the air and yelled, "Listen, you pathetic excuse for a therapist. I don't owe you any explanation for anything I don't want to discuss. You have done nothing but sit there and nod your head this entire time without giving me any answers!"

Paul sat forward and replied, "It is not my job to give you all the answers. The point is that I help you come up with your own reasoning. I am not your Superman!" Emily sat back and decided to unleash her thoughts about October 15th to Paul.

"I need to understand! Why did that man go to this room and that room and to my classroom and decide to open fire, and I am the only one left alive?" Emily continued as the veins in her head began to emerge from her forehead. She wasn't the only one left alive in her classroom that day, but her mind kept going back to the children she saw murdered, all seven of them.

Calmly, Paul sat back in his chair and started to stare at Emily. Paul was frustrated at this impossible woman. However, he admired her sense of urgency. Making aspects of her life after the shooting made sense, but Emily failed to realize one thing:

"It's not always about you."

"Excuse me?" Emily asked as she felt insulted.

Paul laid his hand on the side of his head. He went into more detail: "This whole time, you have told me about the ghosts affecting your life. The strides you tried to make for your class to help them be more engaged, and you went as far as to pat yourself on your back for your ingenuity. The keyword is 'your,' and maybe you should tell me about them. Tell me something real, for God's sake! It's okay if you don't come out smelling like a daisy all of the time."

He's right. Emily knew deep down that Paul was correct. She was so concerned about coming off as the insane one. She was subconsciously talking about her successes in life and not her failures.

Paul thought it very impressive the strides she had made in her life over the past year and a half, but that didn't tell him who she is as a human being.

"Tell me about the last teacher-student conference you had before the shooting." Paul inquired.

The parent conference was one of the last significant moments in her life before things changed, and it wasn't one that she was necessarily proud of.

2

"Okay, kids," Emily began the day in early October of her second year with her students. It was almost halfway through fourth grade, and around this point last year, Emily was sat down to be told she would be taking her class from third grade to fourth. While Emily never told anyone about moving with them to fourth grade, Emily wondered if she would be taking them onto fifth grade as well. "Good morning!" she exclaimed to her class.

"Good morning," they replied.

"Okay," Emily continued, "Sign it."

The students began to bring their hands to their chins as they lay their other hands flat in front of them. Then her students brought the back of their hands down onto it. They put their hands flat inside their arms above where the forearm and upper arm meet. They all brought their lower arms up like they were mimicking the sun rising in a synchronized motion.

"Speaking of the sun rising, what do they call Japan?" Emily asked.

Ava brought her hand to the air faster than Emily had ever seen from her before.

Emily pointed to Ava, signaling her to answer.

"Um," Ava began as she sniffled and pushed up her glasses, "The land of the rising sun?" Emily smiled and asked, "Was that the answer or a question, Ava?"

Turning her head around to see that the entire class was watching her, Ava gave Emily a stern look and replied, "Answer."

"That's right!" Emily exclaimed. She was so proud of her little bug coming out of her shell a bit more every day. It helped that she and Sloane started becoming closer and closer since the previous year.

"Okay, now say it to Feng, please," she instructed.

The class then said, "Ohayō Ggozaimasu!"

The smile on Feng Song's face made it all worth it for Emily. Emily proceeded to start the day with some light reading and math, going by her curriculum. Still, there was no rule stating that she couldn't do more. Emily had already implemented the sign and foreign language portion into her routine despite what Principal Dean wanted. He couldn't argue the positive effect, so he allowed it to happen regardless of county rules. As usual, the noise-canceling headphones were assigned to someone. This time it was Sloane Chastain's turn, and like always, she scoffed at having to do it with her high and mighty attitude.

As the day went along, Emily looked at each one of her students. She wondered if anyone could move on from what some would classify as a remedial class, even though that wasn't the technical classification. For the past few months, Emily Sinclair decided to give her class brain teasers to see if anyone in the class was up to the task of doing some critical thinking. So far, there had been no takers, but Emily wasn't sure if it was from a lack of knowledge or if the students didn't want to be called.

"For today's brain teaser…" Emily began before moaning and groaning came in on cue from the kids.   *Oh, man! Jeez! This again? Uhhhhhhh…so hard!*

"Yeah, yeah," Emily mocked the class.

The kids laughed because of Emily's over-the-top impression of her class. It was a sight to behold as she contorted her face like a whiny child and let out a "wah," only an elderly woman would belt out.

"Anyway," Emily began again, "Here is the riddle: There is a moving crew pulling up a piano into an apartment window because someone is moving in. The rope starts to come apart, and there is a person right underneath where the piano would fall. Right when the piano started to fall, a man across the street yelled, 'Look out!' Later that man was arrested. Why?"

The entire class looked at one another, confused. Derek was the first to raise his hand and ask, "Why would someone get arrested for helping someone?"

Emily shrugged her shoulders and replied, "That's what you have to figure out. In fact, I want each of you to take a few minutes to think about it and write it on the back of the assignment we just finished. Emily gave the class more time than she initially thought because she didn't want time to be a factor and make them nervous. As she scanned the room, she found Bo to be the one who put down his answer. *Not the first person I would have thought to have a good idea this soon.* That wasn't fair of Emily to think, and she knew it. It was social profiling because of the old redneck cliché that is wrong more times than not. The banality came from being raised in the south and then moving to the Midwest for college, making Emily realize that there were many backward-thinking people in her hometown. However, that didn't mean everyone from the south was. However, Emily wanted to be incredibly wrong and see Bo be more than he, or others, thought he was.

Soon everyone set their pencils down and stared at Emily, waiting for her to instruct them.

"Okay, let's hear them! Who wants to start first?"

No child in the room made a move or a sound.

"Okay, let me put it this way: either you start volunteering or pick at random."

"He was a drug dealer!" one student said.

"No."

"He was jaywalking?" Brad answered, unsure of himself.

"No."

"Selling illegal copies of movies," Feng said in his accent.

"Nope."

"He was a pimp selling some hoes," little Ava Nauling said in her tiny voice as she battled a cold. The class laughed.

"No! Jeez! Where…I mean, how do you even know those terms?"

"My parents have HBO. They talk about Pimps Up, Hoes Down sometimes," Ava replied, looking at Emily through her thick pop-bottle glasses.

The answers came at Emily so fast she found it hard to keep up with all the strange and hilarious things the kids spouted out. As she looked over to Bo, Emily couldn't help but notice he was erasing his answer. He was the only one not participating. After asking for her students to pass their assignment papers forward, Emily made especially sure to look out for Bo's and hopefully identify what he wrote down as an answer. Bo Gentry was an honest kid as far as Emily knew, and any hint of shadiness on his part would come as a surprise; Emily just wanted to know why.

After picking up the papers from the ends of the desks, she thumbed through them until she saw Bo's article. Bo was looking at Emily through the side of his eyes; he knew through the looks that Emily was giving him throughout the mind-bender question. She pulled out his paper and flipped it over. As she suspected, the pencil indention was apparent, and he did have the correct answer.

Emily walked over to Bo Gentry's seat and leaned forward to whisper, "I want to see you during recess."

The class let out an audible gasp, "Ooh...he's in trouble!"

Emily turned her whole body around toward the noisy class, "All right! That's enough." Bo's eyes showed disappointment because he was going to have to miss recess. That and Ms. Sinclair would oust him, and he didn't want to have to deal with it.

3

"So, what was the answer to my question I asked earlier, Bo?" Emily said, standing above him with her arms closed like a disappointed parent. Bo wrote on the paper in Emily's hand, and he knew he couldn't get away from it. "Why did they arrest the man across the street that helped save someone?"

Bo sighed and looked away from Emily to stare at the artwork on the wall across from them.

"Because he w.., not bl...d," Bo muttered.

Emily poked her ear forward and asked, "Can you repeat that, please, without it sounding like you have a sock in your mouth?"

"Because he pretended to be blind, okay! The man was arrested because he was blind, and if he actually were, he wouldn't know the piano was about to fall. You can't pretend to be blind. It's like, you know, illegal."

Emily's face brightened, filled with excitement as she discovered that one of her students was more than they appear, but nothing prepared her for what came out of Bo's mouth next.

"There's something wrong with that answer and maybe the riddle. It ain't as simple as that," Bo said matter-of-factly.

Emily raised her eyebrow at him and asked, "How so?"

"Well," he began, "There ain't no law sayin' you can't go down the street with a pair of dark glasses and a cane. You got to be registered and receiving money from the state and all. So really, it would depend if he were skimmin' money from the taxpayers. Otherwise, it's ain't illegal."

Dumbfounded, Emily stared at Bo, the boy with the chubbiest cheeks on the planet, in awe. "I think it is safe to assume that the man registered himself as blind," Emily clarified.

Determined to prove that Bo was smarter than he let on, Emily dashed to her desk and pulled out an old math test that Bo had failed days prior and then another copy of the same test. "I want you to retake this test, Bo, and I don't want to see another failing grade. You have twenty minutes." Emily placed the paper flat down and put a pencil next to him.

Bo took the pencil, sighed heavily, and proceeded to take the math test over fractions. Time went by, and Emily occasionally glanced over to see the progress he was making.

A pencil's sound hitting the desk woke Emily from the trance she had for the last five minutes. She had dreamed about her wedding day and all the accouterments that filled in; it was a little uneven, but she would figure it out.

"I'm done," Bo said with attitude; he was mad he couldn't play with the other kids. It was strange that he was angry at not being in a social situation where kids consistently made fun of his weight and appearance.

Emily scanned through the questions quickly but made sure to check herself in the process. Her eyes made it to the end of the paper, and she realized what she assumed all through the day so far was correct: Bo Gentry appeared to have no business in her class, and it was time for him to move on.

"These are all correct," she stated to Bo, who was staring out the window at a tree whose leaves were turning orange. "You got them all right," she reiterated.

Bo replied, not looking away from the window, with a degree of snark, "I know. You can only say the same thing so many ways."

Emily sat back on her chair and took a deep, frustrated breath, and said, "All of this time? This entire time you have been hiding this. Why?"

Bo shrugged his shoulders as children do when they are trying to avoid the question. "You are so smart! Why do you hide this? I don't understand. You have so much potential to be better and different than some."

Bo jerked his neck toward Emily and yelled, "I don't want to be different!"

Emily began to yell back as a defense mechanism but instead composed herself. "Why? What's wrong with that?"

The large boy shrunk down in his seat and appeared to Emily like the fragile boy she had always seen; his eyes were watering, and his face began to turn red.

"I've seen what different gets ya. It gets adults to wonder what is wrong with ya. Why aren't you more like them? They make fun of ya when you look different, something you can't help," Bo explained before he cried, "I don't want to be like others. I just want to be normal and not be made fun of by people! I'm not queer. I'm not!"

Emily took his hands and whispered, "I know you're not, hun. It's okay, but there is nothing wrong with being smart."

Bo sniffed and replied, "Then, you don't know them."

The only set of people that "them" probably meant was Bo's family. Despite knowing that it could lead to disaster, Emily Sinclair took it upon herself to schedule a conference with them.

4

It was time for a bathroom break for some of the classes at Marie-Glen Elementary. Instead of worrying about a child going to the bathroom and, from Emily's guess, risk a child falling in the toilet, the school designated certain hours for bathroom breaks. Some classes were assigned around noon and others at one o'clock based on what rooms had a lunch break. It was one of the only times that Emily, Margie, and Jamison could get a conversation.

Emily had to talk about the atrocity that she discovered with Bo Gentry faking getting answers wrong due to his anxieties about how his family treated him.

"Can you believe that?" Emily asked.

Both Margie and Jamison stared at her blankly and then came back into reality. "I have to admit, that's unusual for sure," Jamison said, "But I suppose it makes sense to him?"

Confused, Emily squinted her eyes and scoffed, "How does that make sense? What child just accepts to be dumb? Less than what they can be? What parent doesn't want their child to do better than them?"

Margie shook her head and explained, "It's not about that, necessarily. It's the possible realization that you didn't do well enough in life, and then here comes this child to prove you wrong, maybe make you feel inferior. Maybe Bo knows that's what will happen, and he won't have that connection to his folks he wants. Hell, honey, what do I know, though? I am not in that situation. Never have been. My point is that maybe you see this from the wrong point of view."

Margie and Jamison had made sense, bringing their points of view into the situation. Still, Emily could not fathom a world where a child would be made to feel bad for being smart. "Well, I suppose we will see soon enough," Emily said as she noticed Brad Medler, the clown, stepping outside the line to go to the bathroom. The girls in the line started to roll their eyes and say, "Ewwwww!"

"Brad!" Emily yelled with a slight Southern accent, "Get your butt back in the line!" Brad's eyes grew large, and he put out his hands like he typically did before he explained his reasoning. "I was considerate! I had to fart, so I stepped away from the girls!"

"It defeats the purpose when you tell us before you do it, you douche biscuit!" Sloane yelled.

Ha! Douche biscuit. "Sloane!"

The class laughed at the class princess for stooping so low. It was fantastic for them to hear it, and quite frankly, it was great for Emily to hear even though she had to play the adult. It meant that Sloane had the capability of fitting in with others in the future.

"Watch your mouth!" Emily yelled, trying not to laugh audibly.

She saw Jamison and Margie turned around so that the kids wouldn't see their laughter. Jamison composed himself by taking a deep breath and sniffing the snot back into his nose. With a sigh of delight, Jamison asked, "So what do you have planned tonight?"

Sharing in the relief of laughter, Emily replied, "Not sure. Crosby said he had something great to show me when I got home after the meeting with the parents."

Jamison, needing to be the one with a quick joke, said, "Spoiler alert: it's his penis." Emily scoffed and slapped him on the shoulder for making such a funny but unnecessary remark.

There was a secret that Jamison was hiding from Emily, though. He wasn't sure when it began and why it did, but he had become very fond of Emily over the last several months. So much so that Jamison couldn't wait for the day where Emily got tired of Crosby's procrastination on setting an actual wedding date that could lead to her breaking it off with him. Yes, he would be the champion that would be there for her in the end. Jamison knew how conniving that sounded, but he didn't wish any ill will for anyone. Everyone sees a situation as one-sided, and Emily's position seemed to Jamison like she was unhappy. Maybe he could make her happy if given the opportunity. Jamison knew it probably sounded idiotic and was nothing but puppy love, but he didn't care. You can't help how you feel about someone, and Jamison didn't want that feeling to go away.

"What do you actually think it is, though?" Margie asked.

Emily shrugged her shoulders and retorted, "It doesn't matter. I'm sure I'll like it no matter what it is." *That was a lie.* Even though she would deny it, Emily secretly thought it had to do with the wedding or maybe Crosby getting a full-time job. *That would just be so great!*

5

It was a quick turnaround to get Bo's parents to talk about their son and the possibility of him going into a more advanced class. Emily liked Bo a lot. Something was calming about the twang in his voice that reminded her of a boy she was friends with that would visit whenever she visited her grandparents in North Carolina. Maybe it was the idea of a single time in her life.

The final bell had rung about fifteen minutes ago, and that was the usual time any parent meetings occurred. It was easier to get all the students out and onto the buses to make the parents coming into the school more manageable. Most took that as a great courtesy but judging by the annoyed look on Bo Gentry's father's face, that wasn't the case necessarily.

David Gentry was what Emily had expected in her mind. He entered the classroom with a wide stance to help support his weight. From the look of his clothes stained with motor oil and mustard, he had just gotten off work and was none too happy about not being able to go home. *I think I just interrupted his La-Z-Boy time.* Emily felt terrible about categorizing the man without having talked to him. Bo's mother, Glenna, wasn't like her husband in any way. She came off as more of a timid housewife who sat back and watched as events happened in front of her, not saying anything about anything.

"Please have a seat," Emily said as she pointed out the chairs in front of her desk that she borrowed from Margie.

"What happened to him now?" David asked.

Now? Does he usually get in trouble?

"It's actually the opposite, Mr. and Mrs. Gentry," Emily replied.

Both parents looked at each other with confusion; this was a meeting the Gentry's were not used to having. "After going over some tests over the last couple of weeks, it turns out that Bo has no real need to stay in this particular class. He's able to move up to another class level," Emily explained.

"How do you figure?" asked David as he glanced at his wife. There was a level of uneasiness that filled the room. Emily looked over at Bo, who was on the other side of the classroom near the door, and asked, "Can you step outside for a bit, Bo?" She knew that this meeting may not go down the way she intended it wanted it to and that it would be best for Bo not to get caught in the crossfire. Bo nodded his head and walked outside the classroom. He decided to sit on the floor in front of the lockers. He knew the conversation that was about to occur.

"No," David said, "I think he's fine where he is."

Emily squinted her eyes at Mr. Gentry with her mouth hung open in disbelief of what she was hearing.

Glenna chimed in to help diffuse the frustration between the two before it got any worse. "I think what my husband is saying is that Bo, on a mental level, isn't prepared for that type of move and the work it will take to keep up."

Emily sat back in her chair while tapping her fingernails on the top of her desk. What she had feared about Bo's parents was coming to light, and with her quick temperament, she was fighting back to words she really wanted to say. "And how would you know that exactly? Bo just sat here today and did the replacement tests without warning and aced all of them! He was pretending to be less than he is when it comes to his intelligence."

David sat up in the seat and groaned, "Look, Ms. Sinclair, we get that your job isn't easy and all that, but what happened is that you gave a test to a boy who knew how to do the problems after he failed. That's all. You are making a mountain out of a molehill with this."

"Mr. Gentry, I know all of this is sudden, but if Bo is smarter than we realize, then it's up to us to make an opportunity for him."

Glenna sighed at the positivity that Emily was generating and appreciated it, but she knew her husband all too well.

"No. You are trying to make an opportunity for yourself!" David snapped, "I know all about the weird things you're doing here! Sign language and Japanese words. You are trying to make an opportunity for yourself by making underdeveloped kids learn outside the norm!"

Emily's blood began to boil, but she was not entirely sure if it was because it was partly true or if he was just that ignorant.

"No child here is underdeveloped, sir! One is foreign, another is deaf, and it is important for children to feel included and not secluded with their own thoughts consistently!" Emily exclaimed. David nodded his head and moved up to the edge of his seat in anger while Glenna put her hand on his chest to keep him from doing something idiotic. *I dare you to touch me.*

Emily noticed that there were bruises on her wrists where it appeared someone grabbed her. *That piece of shit.*

"I don't want anyone to lift my boy's expectations! Life is hard enough, and this world can and will eat him whole! I don't want him to be different! I want him how he is! I just want him to have an easy life!" David yelled.

"Mr. Gentry! Do you consider your life easy?" Emily snapped back. She'd had enough with this selfishness he was producing for the sake of his boy. "You are making a decision for your son that isn't yours to make! Why is it so wrong to be better?"

David stood up out of his chair, and Glenna stood along with him like the dutiful wife she was. "Trying to be better in this world leads to disappointment," he replied.

"That's your fear, not his!" Emily pointed out.

David puffed out his chest, and lifted his pants, and had his final words: "Thank you for your time, but I think I'll wait a couple of years for a second opinion."

They say people see red when they reach their boiling point. Emily's limit with people was when they let fear and ignorance get in the way of someone else. On October 14th Emily Sinclair made a mistake that could have cost her a career in teaching.

"Okay," she began her tirade, "Here's your second opinion. You are an ignorant piece of white trash that is so afraid that Bo will be smarter and more successful in life than you are. You are willing to keep him at your level to feel hunky-dory about yourself. I may care about my career a lot, but that doesn't change what I know about that boy. You keep him down, and he will resent you and be a miserable piece of shit like his old man. Think about what you are doing. Now, pretty please, with sugar on top, get the fuck out of my classroom before I call social services to investigate any domestic violence that may be going on in your home!"

David and Glenna Gentry stormed out of the classroom. David went over to Bo and lifted him up by the ear, and yelled, "Come on, boy! We're going!"

Bo looked at Emily and back at his parents, confused about what had just happened.

"You are going to pay for that, missy," David yelled at Emily. "I am pretty sure the principal won't appreciate how you talk to parents and give false hope to children."

Emily sardonically smiled and waved at him and replied, "Be sure to blow it out your ass on your way out. You overweight piece of shit!" At that moment, Emily realized that her mouth might have cost her this job. All Emily's efforts over the last year and a half with her students, her kids will have all been for nothing. At least that's what she thought.

6

"Bo's the last one I saw," Emily told Paul as she ended her story about her career-breaking decision.

"You mean on the day of the shootings?" he asked.

Emily shook her head and came back from her memories. She had been doing that often: losing herself in her thoughts and shutting out everything else around her. "Yeah. He was there at the fundraising event in the park square outside my apartment. He wasn't the only one. The others were there also," she continued.

"What did he look like?" Paul inquired.

Emily winced, and in a confused manner, answered, "He looked like death. He looked like all the rest."

7

Everything was falling apart. The dark apparitions of Emily's students appeared to her. The pale children with the chattering teeth were getting closer and closer, her landlord died, and to top it all off, she was positive she was losing her mind.

The fundraiser for the families of those slain in the attack at Marie-Glen Elementary was about to get underway. As much as Emily feared the people who would attend, it would be just as bad if she did not appear. *What's the point?*

Emily felt shunned by the community now. No one talked to her anymore and would only acknowledge her with glares using the sides of their eyes. Emily had no real proof of the latter thought as she was afraid to look at anyone; she just felt the looks of disdain. It was her fault for not protecting them, and while that came off as conceited on her part, Emily was convinced that it was the way others saw her.

The outside looked more like a carnival than an actual fundraiser; it was a more upscale version of what the school district did once a year to help with supplies. There was a small Ferris wheel, a child roller coaster for the little hearts out in, and the famous Gravitron ride. As Emily aptly named it, The Throw-Up Whirly Thing Contraption. Emily knew that it was meant for a good cause. Still, the conspiracy theorist in her wondered if the county was going overboard by promoting the small suburb too much.

She was alone in the empty building where she lived; her love left, her sweet landlord had passed, and all the merchandise in her store was slowly disappearing. There is black, white, and Emily had to deal with the dead children that represented both; "The Pales" and "The Dim." While her sanctuary was coming apart, other ghosts began to appear, trying to penetrate her home and sanity. Emily viewed the outside of her large living room window. She looked in every direction to see if The Dims and The Pales were lingering. *It probably doesn't matter. They will just show up anyway.* There was no end to this tortuous maze and no light at the end of the tunnel. The hate and self-loathing would always be around for Emily; she was sure of it. Hope was gone from her life. She just had to accept that her mind was broken. No matter how many people tried to convey sympathy by telling her it wasn't her fault, Emily knew that the children's deaths could have been prevented. Emily wasn't sure how, but there had to have been a way. Emily was sure of it. This thought tortured her every day since the shooting, and she couldn't let it go.

Emily slowly descended the stairs to the outside. *This is not going to go well.* If anything was to be guaranteed based on the last couple of weeks, this was a given. All she wanted to be was for Crosby to be around now. He always had a positive perspective on events and people. Crosby was sensitive; at least that's what his friends told him that one time he went ghost hunting in Indiana. He was the kind of guy who drove Emily mad, but it was also what she loved about that man; he never backed away from doing something new. Emily was the opposite as she never had that urge to do something out of the ordinary. However, she didn't have a choice now as strange events were happening to her.

She looked around the side of the building when she ambled outside. *Where are you? I know some of you are out there.* The crowd was beginning to form as the day started to end, and for an hour, Emily kept her back against the brick wall of her building, watching people as they gathered, talked, and laughed. *How can you laugh? How can you have a good time? An event to amuse you at the expense of dead children.?* This made Emily sick.

Emily finally emerged from her hiding corner across the street from the fundraiser. The lights and the nip in the air made it lovely in her mind. Then as she got closer to the square, the noises began to bother her. The roar of metal on metal from the roller coaster made her flashback to the past. She remembered the door opening and the end of a shotgun poking through it. The children screaming on the Tilt-A-Whirl brought her to a standstill. The sounds of her students yelling for help as they fled for the back door of the classroom filled her mind. The local competing radio stations and the blaring music mixed with commercials at once confused her. *Now I'll never dance with another. Oh, when I saw her...KSHHH...make an appointment with someone who can help. Dr. Cusick has helped many poor souls.... KSHHHHHH...standing there.*

It was too much to handle as a ringing sound was in her ears. She sat on a nearby bench and shut her eyes, trying to tune out the noise and focus on something else. The sound of laughing children started to ease her anxiety. It seemed like a lifetime since she heard a child laugh. When she opened her eyes, she watched several small children laughing in a group.

The cackling began to slow. The children started to sound maniacal as they pointed at something in front of them.

Emily squinted her eyes to find what the children found so funny.

Look at the fatty! He's so gross! Their voices sounded like an audiotape that had been slowed down. It was happening again like she knew it would: time slowed, and it would inevitably be one of her deceased students visiting her. There was no sanctuary anymore where she would feel safe from her mind and visions. Emily always thought that the word "vision" had a positive connotation, but she had learned that it was also a curse.

The boy that Emily tried to help during his last days was standing in front of the merry-go-round. While the children who lived were laughing with a demonic tone, a massive cloud of darkness was revealed, making them slowly run away. Something was different this time around as the ghost of Bo Gentry looked around his surroundings in sorrow. White dribble was emerging, g from and flowing, down his mouth as he looked down at a white glob on the ground.

Bo put his hands out in front of him. He looked at the black mist emerging from him, covered in the white-painted onto his hands.

Emily didn't want to be seen. But like any human that has seen disaster, she couldn't peel her eyes away from it. Their eyes met, and each looked at one another to make sure the other was real; one of them wasn't in this reality.

The chubby boy she once taught brought his hands outward and began to walk toward her quickly. Swaying, Bo began to speak to Emily, but the words were hard to comprehend. "*Ou use?*" Bo mumbled as his walk lurched into a jog.

Emily fell to the ground and pushed herself away with her legs scooting across the grass. *No! Not again!*

"*Ms. Sinclair!*" he yelled. His voice was disjointed with a low tone like the rest of them as he ran, seemingly confused while excited.

Clack-clack-clack.

No. Not them too! Something forced Emily to face the ghost of her student.

Now the Pales were closer to her than before, chattering their teeth with smiles plastered on their ghostly faces. As Bo approached her, the other children suddenly appeared near the cotton candy stand began to put out their hands, wanting her attention.

Emily put her hands over her ears. She leaned against the quad bench near her apartment. "What do you want? I can't help you! Leave me alone!" she screamed, but as far as anyone else knew, she was yelling into the night sky. That may have been a concern, but no one seemed to care, just like the past weeks.

Bo leaned over Emily's body and whined with his now low-toned voice, "*You see! Nothing changed! Nothing ever changes! No one cares! They still pick on me!*"

Emily screamed as she chose to ignore his plea. "Please stop," she whimpered, "You're not supposed to be here."

White liquid began to drip onto her, but she couldn't feel it because it wasn't real, at least not to her. Breathing in and out at a medium pace would put her into a panic attack. So, Emily attempted to take solace that he was alive in another way and was not frightened. As she closed her mouth to breathe through her nose, Emily caught a whiff of vanilla. *Vanilla ice cream, maybe?*

"*NO!*" Bo yelled. It made the ground under her tremor. He pointed at her. "*You aren't supposed to be here! You need to leave! Isn't there somewhere better? There has must be! Just go!*"

"*He was right,*" Emily thought as she pushed herself against the ground with her feet, "*I do need to go, but I'm not sure how!*" Emily managed to bring herself to her unsteady feet and quickly walked away from Bo as he cried out for her.

"*Why? I don't understand!*" Bo began to follow her.

Emily didn't understand, and as the set of pale white children continued to point at her. Simultaneously, as she moved, all Emily could think was, "*I don't understand either.*" Shortening the distance between them both, Bo began to glide faster towards her. Emily glanced behind her and saw that he no longer had a visible lower torso but was still moving toward her quickly. *I must look ridiculous, a crazy lady screaming into the air being chased by nothing. That's how everyone sees me, I bet.*

Emily burst through the door leading to the stairs of her apartment. Knees weakened, she managed to fall into her bed that she had not been in for days and hid under the blanket.

Knock.

Her mattress and sheets felt like Emily hadn't been to sleep for weeks. When she fell onto the bed, the dust shot upward and filled the room where the. The sheets were cold and stale. Despite it all, it was the safest she felt, like when she was a child and frightened at the dark image at the end of the hallway that was nothing more than a coat rack.

Knock. SLAM! SLAM! SLAM!

The sweet, chubby boy had turned into a vessel of rage. After a minute, the consistent knocks on her front door began to stagger. It wasn't just Bo's hard knocks as, but lighter blows followed. Then Emily started to hear beats from all parts of the door. Some in the middle, some higher up, and some along the bottom. *There are more out there. It's not just Bo banging at my door; it's all of them.* Emily wasn't sure if they were trying to torture her mind on purpose or if they had more to say, but it didn't matter as she wanted nothing more to do with it. They were gone, shot by a man in a mask, and nothing more could do. *It wasn't my fault*, her mantra, to keep any sanity left.

The bumping of tiny fists halted suddenly, and Emily stayed under the covers for a few more minutes before she emerged from her bed. Slowly opening her bedroom door, she peeked down the hall to see if any of them made it inside her home. There was no sign of any of them, just the light shining in the kitchen.

Unconcerned, Emily tip-toed down the hall. She passed her kitchen that was off to her left, not wondering why she left the lights on in the first place.

There was someone in her kitchen, hiding in the corner where the wall and the refrigerator met. With her grey skin flaking off, a woman turned her head around to watch Emily pass by with her back to her.

Emily slowly approached the door and placed her right hand against it; the door was warm. She looked out the peephole and saw the black smoky residue dissipating. *They're gone.* Emily sighed in relief but couldn't resist looking out to watch the blackness fade away.

Emily heard the sound of someone short of breath from the kitchen. Emily jumped and turned her entire body around to face the living room. Too scared to shift her eyes to the left, Emily nervously said, "Hello?" Something was moving around in there; there was no doubt in Emily's mind.

Sssss...Ugh!

Someone was in pain in Emily's apartment, and it wasn't her. Emily moved her body slowly toward the light. Emily thought she saw what may have been a shadow coming out of the entryway to size up what she was about to view; there wasn't. She heard a slight whimper.

CLACK!

Something hit the red linoleum made to look like a brick design on the kitchen floor. The floor of Emily's Emily began to see the kitchen floor emerging into sight as she slowly walked over. There was something on the ground, squirming. It was moving, bending forward a finger that had been cut off. It moved like it was indicating for Emily to come closer. *Come here.*

The woman was facing away from Emily when she came into full view of the kitchen. Grey skinned with blood-tattered clothes on, Emily could see belt marks around the woman's slender neck. Emily knew who it was but refused to believe that one more spirit stalked her after all this time. She had to come face to face with it, her, one more time.

"Do you still bleed?" the woman asked Emily.

Emily's mouth hung open, wanting to speak, *but how do you talk to a dead person?* "What do you want, Rachael?" Emily frightenedly demanded. The dark children, the whites, and now Rachael McKay, the teacher that everyone loved to hate, haunted her.

Rachael cried, *"I wanted not to bleed anymore, but now I want to again. I try, and I try, but I can't bleed anymore."* Emily grabbed the nearest weapon she could. There happened to be a hammer Crosby was using to build before he left, not realizing that it wouldn't protect her in her ongoing battle with the supernatural.

"Get out! No-n-no one wants you here!" Emily yelled.

Rachael brought her head up, ready to turn her ghostly body toward Emily. *"I know,"* she whispered before she began to sing a haunting rendition of, *"Nobody likes me, everybody hates me. I guess I'll go eat some worms."* It was a popular song the children at school used to sing at times.

Emily heard it regularly in the halls but never thought Rachael would care enough about it to remember it, even after death.

"Do you bleed still?" Rachael whispered in emotional pain as her head faced Emily, and the rest of her body turned slowly around. The sound of bone rubbing against bone as Rachael twisted her vertebrae to face Emily echoed in her ears. The kitchen light began to flicker, and when it briefly went dark, Rachael would appear closer than before when it came back on. It was the horror films that scared Emily to come to reality.

Fed up and full of rage, Emily stood up straight with the hammer ready to be swung.

"Yes! I still fucking bleed!"

Rachael turned around. From when she hung herself, the embedded marks around her neck began to ooze embalming fluid, and worms began to creep out of her ears and nose. *"Are you sure? I thought I could. You are a lot like me, Ms. Sinclair…Emily. I just want to feel alive! Can you help me feel good again?*

Rachael moved her arms outward with a pair of titanium scissors to show Emily the cuts she made to herself with her left hand. She was missing a finger from her body's decomposition. Rachael's decaying digit had fallen to the floor from her dead hand. Having inched its way towards Emily's feet, the severed finger created a thick slopping sound. It crept along the floor and began to tap at Emily's ankle.

Emily screamed and kicked the finger to the other side of the kitchen. Rachael jerked her body downward and picked up her severed finger. Shoving it into her mouth, Rachael began to sob as she twisted her body. Her back and face were upside down, but her legs and feet were still facing forward. Bent over, Rachael began to crawl towards Emily in an arachnid-like manner. Her back slid against across the floor. Frightened, Emily cowered against the wall outside the kitchen and watched as Rachael's dead face, upside down, repeating, *"Why can't I bleed?"* All Emily wanted to say was, "I don't know!" but the fear within her kept her mouth clenched. She threw one side of her face against the wall to keep from seeing Rachael's contorted body. Emily started to feel trapped, falling to the ground, unable to move as she dreamt about when she could sleep. Rachael was the nightmare version of Emily in that dreamscape; the body twisted and tortured. *Is that how I will eventually be?* Was that what her dreams were trying to tell her? This would be the point in the nightmare when the light would come to save her, but Emily convinced herself that it wouldn't this time, not in her terrifying reality.

"Why can't I bleed!"

With her eyes tightly shut, Emily started to swing at Rachael's disfigured corpse. Emily couldn't feel any impact from the hammer. Hyperventilating, Emily slowly opened her eyes in fear, hoping to see if Rachael's trace had disappeared. *That was more than just a haunting. There is something else going on*, Emily thought. She laid her head against the wall and dropped the hammer to her side. "Jesus Christ. I can't do this anymore. I need to know if I am insane." she said aloud.

There was an eerier silence than usual in the apartment. No creaking from the building and no heater had kicked on, just the sound of the refrigerator running—nothing else.

"It's *not over for you yet! There is still time!*" Rachael screamed as she suddenly appeared in Emily's living room. She was floating in the air as her bones broke, and her body contorted into unnatural stances. "*Oh, God! I'm burning! It's so hot! Fucking help me! I'm burning alive! Jesus Christ! Help me! I'm in Hell!*"

Rachael's hands combusted into flames first before it spread to the rest of her body. Emily watched as her fellow teacher started to burn away. Pieces of Rachael flew away from her body like embers burning when the wind catches them. The edges of her body turned black and began to crumple together and disappear. Listening to her screams, Emily put her hands over her ears and rocked back and forth, sighing the chorus from one of her favorite songs, "It's all right. I'm okay. I think God can explain."

With alligator tears covering her eyeballs, Emily looked at the ground to see what was left of her former peer: spots of gray sludge and burned hair. Lying on the ground, Emily didn't have the energy to stand up. "It won't go away," she muttered to herself before weeping, "I'm losing me. I-I-I'm losing me." People pray for a better life, for themselves and others, for someone they know, and for help. But no one ever admits that they do it to avoid seeing the wrong places and things that no one talks about. If Emily knew then what she now knew, she would have started praying a long time ago.

"That was the moment?" Paul queried, "That was the moment you decided that you needed help? A vessel for you to become more cathartic?"

Emily knew where Paul was going with this line of questioning.

"Not when you were seeing your dead students. Not when the other children from the school appeared to get closer and closer, but when a teacher you didn't particularly care for comes to you after her death, that's when it's appropriate?" Paul pushed.

Emily nodded her head a little and replied, "When you put it like that, it makes me seem crazier than I already think I am."

Paul leaned forward as if he were about to tell Emily a dirty little secret and said, "Do you know what I think? I think that seeing your students, even though it scared you, gave you comfort that they still exist in some form."

Emily wryly smiled at Paul as she leaned in to reply, "You are absolutely right, Paul. I love seeing the ghosts of dead children. It gives me a rush."

Paul leaned back in his chair to revel in the sarcasm. He liked it when his patients pushed back; it meant that there was life still in them. Emily looked at his leather chair and noticed that it was starting to crack. *When did that start happening?* Everything seemed different from Emily. She noticed that the room's colors were not as pronounced as when she first stepped foot into the office.

"Emily!" Paul loudly said, "Let's keep focus. We don't have a lot of time left." Emily looked back at him as he asked, "Why do you think Rachael McKay burned up? A person already dead, why would her soul—her essence—burn so suddenly?"

Without any hesitation, Emily answered, "Because she was on the clock. Her time ran out."

Paul raised his eyebrow and simply said, "Interesting." Nothing was exciting about it. Emily knew that Rachael's soul went to Hell as it burned her physical form.

Quickly moving on, Paul stood up out of his chair and moved to his desk to lean on it. "Now, it's time to tell me about what happened with Crosby the night before."

"Why do you want to know about that so bad?" Emily questioned.

Paul's facial expression went from empathetic to severe quickly. "It's not for me to know. It's for you to admit and help you move on. As much guilt as you harbor thinking you could have saved some of your students, I think you hold in a great amount of guilt about how your long relationship ended."

Emily looked down at the hardwood floors that now looked stained and knew what Paul was saying wasn't false, but it was still damn hard to admit.

"Okay," she whispered in defeat, "This is it. This is how it happened."

9

On October 14th, after shooting off her mouth before thinking about the consequences, her world started to fall apart. That is what she imagined her headstone would say if left to someone's own devices; "Always Shooting Her Mouth Off." Emily had just self-sabotaged her own career that, at this point, was only in its first year and a half. While she felt saddened by the prospect of not working in Marie-Glen anymore, she wasn't necessarily sorry for it. Emily was never the person to want to give out participation awards because she believed people who work hard should reap the benefits. It was an old way of thinking in this world today, but she didn't believe in it any less.

Walking up the stairwell to her apartment, she saw Claire dusting the furniture in her store. Ms. Dubois waved, and Emily lazily brought her hand up to acknowledge her back.

It was the last day before the tragedy that would occur, and she felt like a failure all around. The only thing that Emily looked forward to seeing was her fiancé, Crosby, telling her that he had a surprise. Otherwise, she would have gotten drunk as soon as she walked through her door.

Emily slowly unlocked the door and nudged it open; it tended to get stuck on occasions, usually when it started to become cold outside. It was October, and the leaves were beginning to change. For Emily, this was always a big deal, but today was not the day to get excited about leaves dying. It was a pessimistic way of looking at it, but it's not entirely untrue in Emily's mind.

She opened the door to find Crosby bouncing around with a goofy grin on his face. For a moment, she felt relief, knowing that he was having a good day for once. Crosby was always the person that was extremely hard on himself in terms of his career and station in life. "What are you so happy about?" she asked Crosby. Crosby grabbed her by the hand and told her to come with him.

He guided her to his office and presented it with a "Ta-da."

Emily looked around and saw that he had put up soundproofing material on the walls and ceiling and some new video and audio equipment attached to a new PC.

"What do you think?" he asked.

Emily stared at the room for a moment and glanced back at him, only to look back around the room with her mouth ajar from shock. She knew where this conversation was going to go.

"What is all this?" Emily asked.

"I created a studio for my voice-over work and any videos I want to create!" he exclaimed. Emily shook her head in disbelief and walked out into the living room.

As she laid her keys in the bowl next to the front door, Crosby followed her down the hall. "I'm excited. It turns out that I am really good at this and could make a nice living doing it, which will help us," he explained.

Emily sighed and scoffed, "No. It's good for you."

"What?" he asked, knowing a fight was brewing.

"Let me ask you a question: Do you just love hemorrhaging money for your crazy ideas?" she asked, "Our money, Crosby! The money that is supposed to pay for our wedding and honeymoon!"

Crosby wiped his brow and retorted, "What you mean is your money, isn't it? This whole notion of being in it together is just an idea with you. Let's face it. You never saw this being mutual in terms of whose is whose."

"Don't pull that sanctimonious shit with me! You have always loved the idea of not having to work for someone else, but this time it has gone too far!" she shouted.

"You have to spend money to make money! That's always the case in business," Crosby retorted.

Emily put her hands on her hips and stared into his eyes with judgment.

"Did something happen at work today?" he asked.

Emily looked away and answered, "Yes, but that's not important at the moment."

"Well, that's typical. You always want me to share, but it's inconvenient when it's the other way around."

Emily walked past Crosby into the kitchen and grabbed a beer out of the fridge. As she turned around, Emily told him, "I told off a parent today, and I'm not sure if I'll have a job soon." Crosby shook his head but was not surprised at what his fiancée did. "Well, that's great. Once again, your redneck mouth got you into trouble and may end up fucking us in the end."

Emily scoffed and yelled, "Oh, fuck you! It's my hard work that lets us live. It's how you pay for all your bullshit, and I have to live with my choices!"

Crosby turned around to walk away but then had a realization. "You know what's funny about all this? You keep on talking about yourself: me, me, me. At no point in our relationship have you hardly used the term "us." But that's just you, ain't it? Always self-involved and not considering the other side. You told me we were in this together, but I don't think we are. I guess I am just the side piece in your life."

"Fine," she huffed, "What's the other side then?"

Crosby took a deep breath. Those next words were going to make or break this engagement. He knew that there would be no going back. "I don't see you. You are always in your work. I never talk to you, and we don't see one another anymore. Maybe if you appeared like you give a shit, this wouldn't have been such a surprise."

Emily grinned and then gave Crosby the deepest of sinister smiles. "You know why I choose to bury my head in my work? It's because what I do matters to people, to them. You are a man with childlike dreams that refuses to grow up. The difference is that at least the kids in my class still have a chance in life. You are too damn old to change."

Crosby frowned. He finally heard what his love thought of him at that moment. Walking away from Emily, he knew what he had to do, regardless of whether he wanted to. Crosby walked into the bedroom and pulled a duffel bag from under the bed and began to pack it with clothes.

"What are you doing?" Emily asked as if she didn't know.

Crosby ignored her and kept packing.

Standing in the doorway, Emily and she watched the only person she ever really loved pack his bag, preparing to leave her. She could have apologized, but Emily was too stubborn for that. Instead, she allowed Crosby to squeeze past her and walk away down the hall.

"Where are you going?" Emily asked.

Crosby stopped before he reached the door and looked at Emily; strands of her brown hair covered her left eye, and all he wanted to do was brush them away. Instead, his hate for her left him just saying his final words to her, "Away from your bullshit."

He slammed the door behind him and stomped down the stairs, not acknowledging Claire dusting her merchandise in her shop. Claire tried to wave Crosby down, but she heard the argument in the apartment above. Looking up at the ceiling above, Claire pondered if she should poke her head in to talk to Emily. Claire shook her head at the idea deciding that it was none of her business. If Claire only knew what was about to happen tomorrow, she would have tried to talk to Emily to convince her to swallow her pride and find Crosby. Unfortunately, hindsight, as they say, is always twenty-twenty.

Emily was left alone, truly alone, for the first time in years, suddenly filled with regret. From literature, she knew that it is regret for the things we did not do that is inconsolable. Still, it's difficult to console the stubborn.

n't Walk Away
Jamie Renee

"You know it's almost time to go," Paul asked before clarifying, "I mean, you realize that we can't stay in this room forever?"

Emily knew that. She wasn't dense, but the idea of what was waiting for her outside frightened her more than her first day teaching her kids. More frightening than the fear of her death or the end of others. With their icy blue-colored eyes and their merciless tendency to following her every move, the children had gotten worse over the weeks. It made her wish for someone to pluck her out of existence. *What do they want? Why me? It's not my fault that you died. I wasn't around you all when it happened!* These are the thoughts that Emily had but never asked out loud from the fear of being ostracized by the community more than she already felt.

"I know," she said as her voice cracked from holding in her tears. Paul sat back in his old chair, twirling his pen that Emily was sure he had a Hawaiian girl in the water. One of those novelty pens usually found in shopping malls is that when you turned upside down, so did the straw skirt. She was sure that if he held it upside down, the plastic girl's hula skirt would flip upside down. Despite his eccentricities, Paul had helped more than Emily would give him credit for out loud.

"I don't have a lot of good thoughts anymore; you have managed to help me feel a bit better. Even if you have been a bit of a condescending ass sometimes," Emily said, giving Paul a backhanded compliment.

"Only a bit?" he said, faking disappointment to make a joke, "I was hoping that maybe I could be a huge ass!"

Emily grinned for a moment before her reality set back in.

Paul leaned forward in his chair as, and it made a creaking sound from the rubbing of the leather. "How do you feel," he asked.

Emily felt like her face had gone numb just from thinking about the answer. How does someone tell a person that the whole day they spent with her was all in vain? What happens to a therapist or a nurse who finds out that everything they did for an individual was for nothing? Emily didn't have what was left of her broken heart to tell her "confidant for the day," Paul Cusick. While it was helpful for a bit, she was still going to go back to fearing her home, and that the anxiety of the shame she put upon herself was still too high.

"It was good talking to you, and I feel better right now," Emily answered to spare his feelings.

"Liar," he whispered.

"Excuse me?"

Paul leaped from his chair toward her body and started to talk aggressively to her. He knocked over the lamp on the end table near her and threw the book off his desk. "You need to say what happened! You must engage your thoughts of that day so that I can help you!" He took her by the arm and pulled Emily toward him. The room began to shake, but she didn't notice because of Paul's monstrous yelling.

"Stop," Emily cried out, "You're scaring me!"

Paul clamped his teeth and grinned. His eyes turned white as liquid emerged from the corners of them. "I can't fulfill my obligations if you don't tell me what happened," he said as his strength and stature grew. Emily pulled away from Paul and stumbled back into the corner as she began to slide down the wall.

The hardwood floors began to break apart as Paul Cusick, the friendly therapist, started to take the form of something else. Something not from this world.

to," Emily yelled, "It's too much. I don't
too scared." Paul took a deep breath as
distorted. Emily listened as he spoke, and
went from English to another, almost archaic
back again. "You have been scared too long now,
ar," he said with a look of slight understanding, "Now
you have to let go and be afraid one more time, and the pain
will go away!"

The walls of his office began to crack through as the floors
separated. Emily looked down beside her to find the founda-
tion had crumbled away, revealing a deep red abyss below.
Lightning strikes came from deep below, contacting the walls
left surrounding them. White lights started to beam in from
the outside. Emily looked out of the window near her to see
the old rustic German aesthetic had disappeared in the gray
mist that lingered outside only to leave a blank canvas.

Wrestling with feelings of nausea, Emily put her hands
upon Paul to push him away, only for her arms to collapse
and give in to whatever force was wearing her down. "My pain
is what keeps me alive," she said, trying to yell.

Paul's hair had turned white, and his eyes transformed into
something monstrous. While Paul's transformation was terrifying to see for Emily, there was a beauty to it that she could-
n't deny.

"No," Paul or whatever being he was, said, "It's what keeps
you alone." Paul put his hands on the sides of her face as she
resisted the feeling of tiredness.

"You don't want this," she said as she started to drift off.

The leftover wood from the floors began to break apart
violently. The splinters started to fly into the air, landing on
both Emily and Paul. Emily thought that small pieces of wood
were going to penetrate her skin. They didn't. The hardwood
floors just disappeared into the air as the room that she
thought was an office faded into nothingness.

"No. I don't," Paul said, "This is what you need."

Emily looked over in a white room and saw the children with blue eyes watching her as Paul put her in a brief trance. Teeth clacking together, the children raised their hands out toward Emily. Emily let out a single tear thinking that the inevitable was about to happen; they finally got their hands on her. She didn't know what would happen when they did. Paul, who was too bright to look at, told her, "Don't worry about them. They won't harm you. They'll get what they have wanted from you very soon."

2

On the 15th of October, Emily remembered the famous mantra uttered by every bored child in the class. Bo Gentry raised his short arm in the air for what he thought was minutes before Emily saw it.

"What is it, Bo?" she asked. In the whiny, let me do what I want, voice, Bo laid it on thick and whined, "I need to go to the bathrooooom!" Emily sighed and decided that he needed testing. She put down the last paint canister on top of the lower shelves in the room to finish preparations for art hour. At this point, the rest of the students usually helped with her class because they wanted to stand, but not Bo. With all his smarts and the diet his parents had eventually put him on, he still wanted to sit.

"Can you not wait for twenty minutes until everyone else goes?" Emily asked her student.

Bo put his hand down and shifted his eyes around in what seemed like a last-ditch attempt to leave class for a few minutes. "Ms. Sinclair," he started his sentence as sincere as

bustin' my grapes? I don't give you a hard
ᵗo leave to do your woman stuff."

ᴸmily was glad that she had a sense of
ᴶ, in Bo's defense, he didn't say "nuts" or
would have been most people's lewd phrasing.
ᴶ got big, as she wanted to show anger but instead
ᴶ it to hold back a laugh. *What did this kid know about woman
stuff?*

Then, in the most innocent, final argument, Bo said, "I
mean, you go all the time during class, and you get paid to do
this."

Emily couldn't argue with that as it reminded her of the
old meme of Elmo on a toilet singing, "My boss makes a dol-
lar, I make a dime …that's why I poop on company
time!" *That should be the slogan for the public-school system.*

"Fine," she said, "but you did not use the magic word, and
just for that, you have to sign it."

Bo rolled his eyes into the back of his head as he raised his
hand to the middle of his chest and made a circular clockwise
motion: "*Please.*"

Emily nodded her head, and he bolted toward the door
like a bolt of lightning.

"Five minutes," she shouted as he left the room.

Emily shifted her focus to the rest of the class heading
back to their seats now that art was over. It was the typical
sight of art time. Sloane put her hair up to make sure paint
didn't get in it. Ava put a red cover over herself because she
finally had an outfit that she felt was respectable. Feng traced
lightly on the paper, so he had an advantage. Jamie Renee
looked out the window at the trees that were beginning to
change color. Brad and Derek schemed, and the rest hinged
on what Emily was going to instruct them to do on that chilly,
crisp day.

A blast of regret came over Emily as she began to remember her fight with Crosby the night before. *I'm not wrong.* That's all she could think about now. Not about his side of the argument, but her final blow in the fight making a valid point.

"Are you okay, Ms. Sinclair?"

Emily looked up and found Brad looking big-eyed, waiting for an answer. Emily shook her head, smiled, and replied, "Fine. I just remembered something. Do you ever have that happen?"

Brad smiled and answered, "Totally. I go into the bathroom to brush my teeth, but when I go in, I forget what I was doing and go back to what I was doing before."

Emily cut her eyes at Brad and simply asked, "You did brush your teeth last night, didn't you?"

It took for a moment for Brad to scoff at what Emily was alluding to. "Yeah. Totally," he answered as he looked down onto his blank canvas. *No, he didn't.*

"Okay, everyone, I want you to take one color of paint— just one as you create something original. After we do that, then we'll trade and create something else on the canvas," Emily said, trying her best to sign for Jamie Renee to understand.

Pop.

Emily paused and looked around to see if the kids had a handheld game system or phone making noise. Emily saw nothing as all the kids were gathering supplies to start painting.

Pop.

It wasn't unheard of that Margie would make popcorn for her students sometimes. Emily marched to the door that was adjacent to her classroom. After slightly knocking, Emily poked her head in and encountered many third-grade faces looking at her. Margie looked up from the book she was reading to the class. "Sorry," she whispered, "Are you making popcorn?"

Margie Furlong shook her head, "Is everything okay?"

"Do you hear that? It sounds like a popping sound. I know it's probably coming from the other side of the school somewhere, but I wanted to make sure my ears weren't playing tricks on me."

Everyone, including the kids in both classrooms, listened to the noise. The noise startled everyone in both classes.

Bam.

Emily looked Margie in the eyes waiting for the same thought she was having, but it didn't come to her. One of Emily's biggest fear as a teacher may be coming true. *I hope I'm wrong. Oh, I hope to God that I'm wrong.*

"Get your kids out the door to the outside," Emily demanded.

Not understanding what Emily was talking about, Margie shook her head. "Kids!" she yelled, "I need you to make a line at Mrs. Furlong's class's back door. The children stood in their place, frozen. It was the first time they heard their teacher yell in a long time. Emily made fists try to calm herself down; it was an old trick her dad taught her when she got worked up.

"You aren't in trouble, kids," she said with tranquility, "It's a drill, and we need to show everyone how good we are at it, but I need you to do it quietly. All right?"

The children in both classes quickly nodded as Emily was oblivious to the third-grade level agreeing with her. As the students walked into Furlong's class to head outside, there was an overwhelming sense that something was missing.

Bang.

At that moment, Mrs. Furlong knew what Emily was trying to hint at without scaring the kids; someone was firing a shotgun inside the school.

Oh shit, Emily thought, *Bo!*

3

"Where are you going?" Margie Furlong asked, rightfully fearing the worst.

Emily stopped at the front of her classroom door connected to Margie's and demanded in a low voice, "Just get the kids to line up in the front of the door to the outside! I need to get Bo!" Emily peeked out to see if the shooter was visible yet, slowly opening the door to the hall. The building was darker than usual on account of the halogen bulbs going out over the month. The district did not want to pay out the money to replace them.

Emily measured the distance from her class to the set of bathrooms. It wasn't far away, but if the shooter were closer than she thought, she would be putting herself and Bo at risk even more. *Maybe he's smart enough that he would lock himself in the stall and then hide.* Bo was intelligent, but she didn't want to count on it because, for all she knew, he could be oblivious to what was going on. Looking at the boy's bathroom, Emily forgot that there was a fire alarm next to the entry. That was it. *I need to kill two birds.*

Emily jolted down the hall as fast and as quiet as she could. To keep herself steady, she put her hands against the grungy blue tiles outside the bathroom entrance that she vowed she would never touch. She slid into the boy's restroom and put her back against the partition that keeps the kids from peeking inside the bathroom from the hallway. After a quick breath, Emily looked around the corner. Bo was nowhere in sight.

"Bo," Emily whispered. She tip-toed into the bathroom and looked around the urinals and the corners. "Bo," she repeated, "We don't have time for this. We need to get outside. Everyone is waiting for you."

Emily's black high heels were becoming a nuisance. The clacking of heels on the linoleum floors of the hallway and bathrooms was too much of a giveaway. Plus, they hurt like hell. Emily kicked them off her feet in desperation; one flew into a boy's urinal with a pink toilet cake that still had urine floating on top. The other hit the wall, which made a loud echo. Emily gritted her teeth at the noise, hoping that it didn't attract too much attention.

As she ran barefoot in the bathroom, she got on her knees and began to look underneath toilet stalls. There were three in all, and by the time she got to the last one, Emily could see Bo on the toilet seat with his knees up to his chest.

"Bo, thank God," she quietly exclaimed.

Bo, cradling his chubby legs with his hands, started to rock back and forth.

"We need to go, buddy," Emily said softly.

Bo shook his head in defiance. "What is happening?" he asked.

"I'm not sure, pal," Emily lied, "I don't want to find out, and we still have time. Please."

Bo rocked back and forth as he hid his head behind his knees. Emily took a deep breath to compose herself. It was time to tell it like it was to Bo, just like his dad previously.

"I know you're scared, but I need you to help me. I can't figure this out or help others without you." Bo peeked over his knees at Emily.

"Okay," she said, "No more bullshit." Emily peered into his eyes as Bo was taken back by her curtness. "You are one of the smartest kids I have known, but you and I can't help others if you don't cooperate. Some people need to know that you are safe. I need to know you are safe."

Bo loosened his grip from his legs, and tears formed over Emily's eyes.

"When you grow up, I know you will be the best person, and you will help people and save them like you always talk about doing, like a superhero. I need you to grow up for a little while and help me save everyone. You are so much more than you think you are. There is something special in you, and I hope I am around to see it when it comes." A pause came between them as another shot was fired somewhere in the school.

"Now I need you to run out of here with me," she said as Bo stood up. "Now…run!"

Bo burst through the toilet stall door, almost hitting Emily in the head with it. She took his hand and ran around the partition to the hallway.

Emily stopped outside the hall as Bo broke away from her grasp to run inside the classroom. The other kids were on their way out of the building. There was a dark silhouette at the very end of the hall where her class was located.

It was the shooter. It was a coward, dressed in black, wielding a shotgun. Emily curled her lip as she placed her hand on the fire alarm on the wall and pulled it down without a single contradicting thought. The sirens rang out, and the rest of the school was now aware that something was wrong. Emily then ran back to her class to find that getting the children out of the school wasn't going as planned.

4

"Why aren't you outside?" Emily yelled.

Margie kept pushing her body against the emergency door in her class that led outside. "It's stuck," she cried as she started to collapse to the floor.

"Then push it open!" Emily shouted at Margie as tears began to swell in her eyes, and she began to see a glimpse of her possible death.

"I can't!"

Another shot rang out from down the hall. Judging from the noise echoing, both Emily and Margie had a feeling in the pit of their bowels that it came from Mr. Harris's second-grade class. *Oh, my God. What do we do now? Oh, no! Jamison!*

Emily still had time. She fixed her gaze towards the back door in Mrs. Furlong's class and noticed that the key was still in the lock. "What is wrong with the door, Margie?" Emily calmly asked.

Margie looked at the children in the class. She suddenly acquired a surge of energy through her body, realizing that this circumstance, this heinous and unjustified act, was not about her safety but rather the students.

"The key," she mumbled as Emily moved her head toward her, "The key is turned, but the lock won't unfasten! The locks are so old that they may be rusted, maybe, or I have the wrong key."

Emily thought back to the time Dean Williams had to open the janitor's closet.

"These locks, I tell ya. They're so damn old that you really must put effort into turning them. I'm afraid that I'm going to break the key off." That's what he said. *It's not the key; it's the lock!*

Emily's recollection of that day's events brought her to her feet and the rusted metal door at the back of the room. She grabbed the key and turned it to the right as hard as she could. Gritting her teeth, Emily yelled as she used all the strength in her hands and wrists to get that lock open. It didn't work, but she could feel the lock wanting to move.

Again, Emily gripped the key and turned as hard as she could, making her hand bleed and blister. "Come on," she exclaimed, "Not today!" The bolt holding the door in place began to budge. She could almost hear; she wanted to hear, the rust rubbing against metal as all she wanted was to hear and feel it move just a bit more.

Clack!

Emily fell backward as the door handle flew forward. The air began to blow inside the classroom. Graded papers on Furlong's desk started to blow off. The children's artwork painted on cheap construction paper began to flail.

"Come on, kids, we need to get outside!" Mrs. Furlong demanded. Emily got on her knees and watched her kids leave one by one. There was a sense of calm that surrounded her. She looked at the finger paintings on the wall of the classroom. As she watched the final student from her class hop down onto the grass going toward the playground, there was a dread that something was missing as her moment of serenity dissipated. She looked at the pictures, the art and felt the need to get back her feet to look inside her classroom again. She peeked inside her class as most of Margie's class had gotten out, and Emily's were on their way.

There was a girl in the front corner of the room, at the art station. It was Jamie Renee. She didn't know what was happening. A person in dark clothing and a ski mask walked into the classroom as Emily dashed towards Jamie. She fixated on choosing the right colors for her painting. As Jamie placed the red paint jar on the table, her potential killer pointed their shotgun toward her pink blouse. Emily reached out to her, yelling Jamie's name as if she Jamie could hear her. Six of Emily's students ran back into their classroom, looking for their teacher, only to find a dark silhouette holding a shotgun towards their friend. Multiple blasts, and red, like the color of blood, were the last things that Emily could remember about that day.

The loudest sounds are the ones that resonate with us the most: a bold child, a coach, a teacher, or a line from a film. The blast from a shotgun was the sound that haunted Emily's life after that. Not her childhood, not her teachings in life, not the singing from her fiancée, but a weapon used for the worst evil imaginable...the murder of children. On October 15th, Marie-Glen Elementary went into history as one of the worst domestic terrorism events on U.S. soil.

The Best Intentions

"Are you the devil?"

That had to be it. In Emily's mind, there was no other explanation. She was never a religious person, but she did know from Catholicism that Hell was continuously where the dead repeated their worst moments from their lives. The man who was supposed to be there to listen and give advice was a being of a coherent mind that brought back her nightmare. Emily believed that Paul was an evil overseeing the torturing of her mind. He was not.

With her hands over her face, Emily hoped that her classroom was no longer present and the possible images of children's deaths not surrounding her. Emily heard someone walking toward her. The sound of footsteps walking over water echoed in the room, whatever room she was in now.

"The Deep Fall is where the bad, selfish, and evil go to view their wrongs for the rest of eternity. You aren't any of those, Emily. I am not the devil. I hope that I am far from it," Paul replied.

Emily felt his hands on hers, gently trying to pull them away from her face.

"Deep Fall?" Emily questioned.

Paul snickered and said, "Yes. It's not a place you have to worry about. You will never have to see it."

Emily's hands still refused to move from her face.

"However, you need to understand what is happening and accept the truth of your life." Shaking her head, Emily refused to uncover her eyes. "It's actually kind of lovely here," Paul said in wonderment, "I come here sometimes just for time to myself. I tend to have a busy schedule, so when I get the time, I come here to The Calm."

Paul was never a celestial being that got impatient quickly. What kind of messenger would he be if he yelled all the time? In this case, Paul was beginning to get impatient with Emily. He understood the turmoil of the situation, but this was about more than just her.

"I need you to trust me now, Emily. I know it's hard, but there is more at stake here besides just you."

Emily leaned over with her head and hands facing the ground that was now wet with a thin layer of what she assumed was water. "I don't want to be here anymore," she yelled.

Paul sighed and replied, "You don't even know what, or where, here is."

Emily looked through her fingers for a moment to see blue and green hues of color around her.

"I need you to look at me, Emily," Paul requested.

Emily still didn't move from her position, and her murmuring sounds were the only sound in the area; *This isn't real. I just want to forget and move on. It wasn't my fault they died. I could only do so much. Nothing worked in that school, not even the locks. What was I supposed to do differently? Why does everyone hate me? It wasn't my fault.*

Emily kept telling herself that the tragedy in Marie-Glen Elementary wasn't her weight to bear, and she was right, but she didn't believe it. Her students—her children—were dead, and all Emily could think about was how she could have saved them. Emily couldn't move on with her life in whatever direction it would take her because of her conceitedness. It was vain to think that an event could have changed anything if they did something different. Maybe that is what Hell was. Perhaps she created her version of it without knowing it.

Paul, and others like him, were used to this notion of arrogance from humans: humanity and their delusions of self-importance.

Still muttering to herself, Paul used a voice from deep within to get Emily to pay attention to him. "Look at me!" His voice compelled Emily's body to do things against her will. Her hands and arms flew back behind her as her chest pointed toward the sky. She couldn't move anywhere except her eyes that started to wander around the space between Heaven and Earth.

The place they were both in was dark, with a floor that rippled. Blue and green bulbs of light floated around, illuminating the room so that a person could walk the area with ease. It was beautiful and was one of the most calming and divine moments in Emily's life, aside from the paralyzing effect. throughout her body as

Paul approached her, again, as the floor rippled with every step he took.

"I should probably apologize for every terrible thing you have seen today," Paul said, "It's not fair. It's not fair to be subject to a moment in time that was terrible for you and the way you remember it. However, you needed to start realizing the truth about actual events things."

Emily started to regain control of her body slowly, as she lingered on every word Paul was saying. Paul took her by the hands and helped her to her feet. Struggling to find the words, Emily stuttered, "Wha...what...what truth?"

Paul smiled and replied with a grin, "That not everything you believe to be is true actually is." Standing alongside Paul, Emily couldn't make out what he was trying to say. Each step they took into the darkness without end, the floating bulbs rose higher from the ground, making the room open into a wilderness. Emily no longer felt trapped in the dark, as some of the lights from the ground became brighter and even merged, giving the woods an aqua hue. "What are these?" she asked Paul.

"We call them Lumes; they pave the way for those with the greatest intentions in life and those that go above the ordinary."

Taken back by its beauty, Emily forgot for a moment that the supernatural occurrence she was witnessing was atypical.

"Humans depend on one another in life regardless if they realize it or not," Paul told her, "Sometimes it is small. Other times the thread that binds us together is thick and cannot be broken. Because of that, people can't move on because they refuse to let go and convince themselves of false truths which keep the rest from going on to another life."

Emily and Paul reached the end of a cliff outside the forest. The lights around them turned yellow and orange that illuminated the sky and the horizon before them. It was like a sunset with no sun in sight. The wind was heavy and blew the lights lingering around them into the sky, only to turn into reds and pinks. New illuminations grew out of the ground, and the cycle started to repeat with blue and greens. Emily was no longer walking on wetness under her feet, but now above fresh, yellow grass. Not the dead grass, but the yellow color you see on a sunflower.

"I don't understand," Emily cried, "What you say doesn't mean anything to me. All I know is that you are something…different. Why did you see me?"

Paul tilted his head and replied, "I didn't. You came to me. Do you even remember how you knew of me?" Emily thought long and hard, thinking back as hard as she could.

"One of the teachers told me about you and said I should talk to you," Emily exclaimed, excited that she thought her answer was correct. Paul shook his head and smiled, "No, he didn't. Mr. Harris simply said that you should talk to someone."

Emily's head started to hurt. She walked away toward the edge of the cliff. Leaning over, she found herself above the clouds.

"I have been in your life for the last few weeks now, Emily," Paul began to point out. "It may have been on a television set, a radio ad, or a grocery store announcement between the unplugged versions of popular pop songs. I have been there talking to you."

Emily faced Paul with her back to the edge.

"Why not just simply call or find me?" she asked.

A fair question, to be sure, and Paul answered honestly. "I couldn't. I am not allowed to initiate the meeting. I had to coax you to find me instead." Emily became frustrated with the answers she was receiving.

Crying, Emily shouted, "Why!"

Paul couldn't answer the question. Emily had to choose her faith herself, and Paul couldn't tempt her one way or the other. It was a directive for all beings like Paul, who look after the people below them, but there was one thing he could say that was vague enough.

"Because you are not the only one dying inside."

The clouds below them started to grow thicker and rise around them, making the pink sky above them hard to view. The blue and green lumes gathered around them so they could see one another as they conversed.

Paul and Emily stared at one another for a few moments...moments that seemed like a lifetime.

"I know that this is hard for you to understand now, but you have to know," Paul sternly said.

With dried tears on her face, Emily frowned, not wanting to know the answer to the question she had to ask, "What do I need to know?"

Raising his hand to her chest, Paul answered, "The difference in what you think and what is real." Suddenly Paul pushed Emily's chest lightly, and Emily fell over the cliff into the thick clouds below them. Emily did not scream. Emily did not cry. She simply watched as the clouds she fell through turned into white feathers. The most beautiful scenery she had ever seen was disappearing every second she fell.

Paul looked down at Emily as she fell. "Time to fall back to Earth," he whispered. Turning his back to the edge, Paul fell backward and followed Emily down to the truth, down to the bottom of it all.

2

No one can avoid it. That dream that everyone seems to have of themselves running through the woods or a field where they are chased by a faceless figure or possibly frolicking through flowers. Suddenly, they fall through a hole in the ground. The immediate reaction is for said person to wake up before they hit the environment because they are startled by the sudden fall, not because they could reach the bottom. Most will tell you the old tale that if you hit the ground or even die in your dream, you will pass away in the real world, but there has never been any concrete evidence. How would anyone know? No one knows what someone else dreamed.

Emily was pushed off the cliff in a world as she had never seen before by a man, no, a being, that she trusted. The feeling of suddenly falling into a dream was apparent in her stomach as those butterflies her parents talked about took over. Like when your parents went over a steep hill in the car at high speed, and the tingles in your belly made you feel funny. That feeling was in her the entire way down. She was sure that she was going to die. Still, if Emily could wake up, she could save herself from the inevitable impact.

As Emily fell, the velocity level grew, and blocks of light traveled past her faster and faster: blues, reds, purples, pinks, and yellows. As she fell faster, the lights began to form images like a child's flipbook. Instead of a penciled character, it was an array of illumination. Forms of animals and flowers came to be, but the tranquil, colorful pictures began to fade. Faces of friends and her students took shape afterward. Voices echoed from the pit below, *"Why? Why are you scared? It's not fair!"* All the voices from her life in Marie-Glen began to yell at her, and the children began to whine as their faces became distorted, *"Tell us, tell us what is real!"* For Emily, this was a nightmare, but when the lights formed the face of her love, Crosby's beautiful face, there was peace. She stared at the lovely colors that made up the outline of his face with all the lines, crinkles, and imperfections. She grinned as she finally got to see her Crosby, even if it was the last time.

"Away from you," the sound of his voice echoed from the depths below. She shook her head, trying to let her voice out of her throat, but she couldn't. Even if she did, Emily wouldn't have known what to say. "Away from your bullshit," was the last thing he muttered to her. That was what she kept in her mind the most, not the good times before, but the last moment before he walked out the door of their apartment. She closed her eyes as she threw her arms and legs back, letting her body go, and becoming one with the momentum of the fall.

Trying to keep herself calm, she was hopeful that it would be quick. Emily had read that most people falling to inevitable death have a heart attack way before impact, but that didn't seem to be the case with her. *Maybe I will just explode when I reach the ground, and I won't feel a thing. Then again, with my luck, I will fall and break every bone in my body and just lie on the ground to suffer. That would be Hell for sure.*

Just when she thought that the hard surface would be the end of her life, she fell into a pool of water. Air bubbles emerged from her mouth and nose as she struggled to swim to the surface. An otherworldly force pulled her down more, like something grabbing her legs and lightly tugging. Emily went from fear of landing on a hard surface to drowning in an unknown abyss.

The water's surface of water lingered above her as she watched the world outside. The beams of color that raced by her as she fell began to disappear. Emily wondered if she was underwater or was just an illusion constructed by her mind. When Paul penetrated the water's surface, she felt a moment's peace before remembering he was the cause of her current duress. A green hue appeared around her, illuminating her descent. Paul, piercing through the water like a submarine, reached Emily and proceeded to float beside her.

"It's okay," Paul said to her plainly under the water. No air pockets left any orifice of his body. Emily glared at Paul, wondering who, what, he was, and the point for these theatrics. For what seemed to be minutes, Emily had wondered if her life was going to end. As she realized her situation, her wonderment lessened. Emily scowled at Paul and emphatically rose her middle finger toward him. If she could have talked, Paul would have heard every expletive Emily could muster. Paul gave a sinister grin towards Emily as she shot the bird because he knew what would happen next.

Something was wrapped around Emily's leg, and it ascended the faster she began to sink. Paul smiled and descended alongside her as her screams, muffled by the liquid, were some of the loudest Paul had ever heard. With the fear reigning over Emily, he continued to smile and silently whisper to her mind that everything would be fine. *It's alright. You're okay.*

Emily looked down at her legs and found blue, leafy vines were wrapped around her. They were not pulling her like she initially thought. Instead, they guided her to the bottom of the spiritual pond. From the cliff high above, Emily fell into it. The leaves started to tickle the depths of her feet innocently. Emily felt the sensation in her arches and felt the need to giggle in the middle of a terrifying situation. Emily squirmed, attempting to break free of the vines that tethered her until she started to notice the surface of the water creeping closer to her; the water level was lowering.

Emily immediately gasped for air when the water descended into the land beneath her. She didn't know that she was never in any immediate danger. The water would have never caused her to drown, but with the suddenness of her descent, it was that detail that Paul failed to mention. The vines guided her feet to the ground and began to disappear. The floor started to fix the holes that the vines created immediately, and the green lights began to dissolve. She was back to the darkness again, and the puppet master, Paul, or whatever his name was, began to walk toward her.

"I told you that it would be fine," Paul stated.

Emily shifted her gaze from Paul to the darkness behind her. Nervously, Emily felt she needed to make a sarcastic comment, "Well, that was a terrible trust exercise."

Paul walked around Emily like a lion hunting their prey, but he was not there to harm her, but to assess if her mind was ready for what was coming.

Emily looked up to Paul's eyes that were now all white. "What do you want from me?"

Paul stopped in front of her and answered, "It's not me that wants anything. It is them that need you," Paul said, pointing to the right of her. Emily looked at all ten children that haunted her through the corner of her eyes. They appeared, forming a circle around her and Paul. The children's teeth chattered louder than ever before. Unlike previous encounters, Emily saw the wounds and dried blood on their bodies. Some were on their chest, one had some on her neck, and another on the side of his face.

"They're cold," Paul stated, still facing her.

"Why?"

"The deceased that have not moved on remain in The Middle, or Limbo, if you prefer." Emily shook her head, disagreeing with herself, remembering all the religious classes and sermons about the afterlife. "I don't believe in that," she said sternly.

"Just because you don't believe the details doesn't mean something doesn't exist in some form," Paul replied.

The children's clacking of their incisors became deafening. The noise soon stopped, and they began to point at Emily. The children opened their mouths and released a piercing wail like a symphony of pain and frustration at once. Emily put her hands over her ears, and the walls that surrounded them began to peel away like chips of paint. The Flakes of black began to float away to reveal a hallway. Emily recognized this hallway all too well; it was the hallway that led to her classroom at Marie-Glen Elementary.

"What is this?"

Paul looked over to her and answered, "What you need to see."

3

The nightmare was happening again.

"This has must be purgatory," Emily thought to herself. *"Why else would something make me watch this again?"*

The hallway was quiet for a moment before the shotgun fire began. The blasts didn't start down the hall; they started right next to them in the room next to Emily's class. The children that surrounded them had now disappeared, and only Emily and Paul were left.

Emily looked ahead, avoiding looking at the shooter and any carnage that ensued in Mr. Harris's second-grade classroom. The door swung open, and the shooter briskly walked past Emily as her hair shifted from the breeze. For the first time, Emily wanted to see their face, but his face was distorted like a television broadcasting dead air when she looked. The shooter headed to her classroom, and Paul took her by the shoulders, inching her closer to view the events.

"Stop!" Emily yelled, "I know what happens, I've seen it! Don't make me do it again!" Paul placed his hands on each side of her face, and with a deep, echoing voice, he yelled, "Watch!" *His voice. His voice could shake the Earth apart.*

Her body grew numb as Paul pushed the back of her neck, forcing her to move toward the door of her old classroom. Emily saw the backside of Jamie Renee, the deaf girl who couldn't communicate with anyone around her for almost a year and a half ago. She calmly chose her paints. The only solace that Emily Sinclair could take out of this situation was that, hopefully, Jamie did not know what was happening behind her and that her death was quick. The perpetrator, that monster that wielded the shotgun, aimed his sights toward little Jamie Renee's back. Suddenly, a person leaped in front of the shooter as their backside faced the end of the weapon.

The person leaping looked seemed familiar to Emily, but she didn't want to know; however, she had to look. Emily couldn't close her eyes if she wanted because of Paul; his otherworldly abilities forced her eyelids open like a vice. For a man that appeared unathletic to Emily at first sight, she was frightened of his strength and the hold he had over her body.

The area around her turned dark. Fate had forced her to watch this atrocity over again.

The shotgun fired, and the impact of the blast hit the person leaping to Jamie's rescue. The blood splattered from both sides of their body, from the back and the chest. Emily couldn't help but see everything in slow motion. Brave people are few and far between, but this person that Emily was watching die in front of her was one of the rare exceptions. When the sound of the woman crashing to the floor startled Emily, the clanging of desks and chairs toppling over one another as she pushed them out of the way to reach Jamie. While Emily's concern for the brave soul on the floor was piqued, her fear was higher for the children.

Jamie Renee stood in front of her paint area. Near the lifeless body that saved her with red all over the back of her dress. It was what Emily had tried so desperately to forget, the death of her students. Regaining some movement of her neck, Paul gently tilted her head a bit in the hopes that she would look to her left. Mrs. Furlong's room was next on the shooter's agenda as the children from both places were trying to get through the door leading outside. *Wait. The kids came back into the classroom! Get them to run the other way!*

As Emily watched, Mrs. Furlong put her arms in the air to block her classroom door adjacent to Emily's. In the back, Emily could see the children shuffling out of Margie's classroom to the schoolyard. *They got out??*

The vile shooter, the coward, the person dressed in black, raised their shotgun to Mrs. Furlong's chest and opened fire. She fell onto her back in the middle of the doorway as she bled out. The children from both classes had escaped, but that's not how Emily remembered it.

Paul loosened his grasp over Emily. Free to move about, Emily pushed his hands away from her, walking toward the woman bleeding on the ground. From her perspective, Emily couldn't see the woman's face initially as the blood from her body had begun to dry onto her hair. As she stepped closer to the body and Jamie Renee, the body's features became all too familiar; the makeup, the eyebrows, and the outfit were all characteristics of Emily. Everything about the body was like her...because it was her.

Emily stared at the version of herself on that fateful day on the floor. The shooter had left the room only to be met outside the classroom by the local police. She began to understand a little about what was happening. *But if I died, then...*

She rose her head to look at Jamie Renee's body, noticing that it had not fallen. It had not wavered. She was still standing in front of the paint area, unaware, not catching that the red paint had splattered all over her from the buckshot hitting one of the canisters. She was breathing. *Oh my God, she is breathing!*

After everything that occurred behind her, Jamie Renee still had no idea that the teacher that taught others her unique language was lying dead behind her. Most people get a feeling that something is in disarray; the air is different, and the sense of something other than yourself is apparent as it occupies the space around you. If one believed in ghosts, there would be an inexplicable feeling of dread that people tell you happens sometimes.

Emily will never know what prompted Jamie Renee to begin to turn her head around after the fact. The scent of gunfire, the lack of vibration on the floor from kids walking in the room. Maybe just the feeling of death around her. Jamie lowered her shoulders, knowing something was wrong behind her.

No. Oh, please, no! Don't let her see me like that! The thought of Jamie seeing a hole in her chest was now the worst thing to happen from this devastation. Jamie began to turn her body around, and Emily closed her eyes. She did not want to see her reaction to the death behind her.

Emily felt the presence of someone beside her. She peeked with her left eye and saw a police officer running to Jaime. The older officer put his hand over Jamie's eyes as he picked her up to carry her out of the classroom. When the officer turned back around, he waited to take his hands away from her face. Unfortunately, it was a bit too early.

Jamie turned her head to find her teacher's lower body twisted on the floor with enough blood next to it to make it visible there was something wrong with Emily.

Reaching her hands out, Jamie spoke, though she rarely did. "Mit Syncare! No! Mit Syncare!" When Emily's real body didn't respond, Jamie screamed as she held on to the door frame, trying to pull herself and the man holding her back in. The officer pulled her little fingers from the doorway, and the cries of sadness echoed through the hall.

Emily put her hands over her ears as the screaming and yelling began to fade away. Mrs. Furlong's body dissipated as well as the mess that the chaos created. The air around Emily grew thick as Paul walked in front of her. At first, there was an immense amount of hate in Emily's eyes towards Paul. He had shown her horrors, but not the same kind that she thought she knew. After realizing that everything she felt did not happen, there was relief instead. It was then that everything began to make sense to her. The silence from others, the feeling of loneliness, and why Paul didn't have a reception area outside his office, like most therapists, have privacy concerns. None of it was what she thought it was. She was never alone. Emily simply died.

"It was paint?" she asked Paul, unsure of herself.

Paul smiled, relieved that it was making sense to Emily now, and let a long sigh as he replied, "It appears so."

Confused, Emily looked around the room as she formulated her questions.

"This is usually the part where the affirmation questions begin," Paul said, inviting her to belt out the questions that she undoubtedly would have. Emily had no issues with asking.

"So. I'm..."

"Dead. Yes."

Emily scoffed and turned away from Paul. "Why didn't you just..." Emily began again. "Tell you?" Paul finished.

Annoyed, Emily yelled, "Knock it off! Let me finish my damn sentences! At least give me that."

Paul nodded in agreement.

"Why not just tell me?" Emily asked again.

Paul began to walk around her as he started to explain. "It doesn't quite work like that. I couldn't just tell you the truth."

"Why?"

"It's just the rules. You had to come to that self-realization yourself to move on. I couldn't come to you. You had to be coaxed to come to me by the others," Paul said.

"The others?" Emily questioned. "Yes, children with white eyes and chattering teeth. They didn't want to do it, but with them appearing and frightening you, it was a way to get you to me. See, they can't move on to the afterlife until you do. You are all connected because of the tragedy that happened at the school."

Emily shook her head, trying to process the information as best she could. "Wait," she stuttered, "How are they connected, exactly?"

Paul sighed and walked toward her, "They were children in your school."

"Yeah," she stammered, "I knew they looked familiar."

Still not understanding, Paul had to put it as delicately as he could. "Emily, not every child, escaped that day."

Emily was obsessed with the notion that her kids died and that it didn't occur to her that others might have. "I feel so ashamed," Emily muttered as she put her hand over her mouth. As much as Paul experienced helping poor souls move on, human interaction was never his strong point. He nervously put his hand on her shoulder to offer some sort of comfort. Emily wedged herself into his chest to cry. Paul put his arms around her slowly as he was almost sure that it was okay for this situation. "They're cold. That's why their teeth chatter. It is very cold sometimes," Paul continued to explain.

Emily pulled away from Paul gently as shea bit wiped her tears away.

"You did pretty well overall!" he exclaimed, "Besides, I am not completely daft. I did a little something to help guide you."

Emily looked up at him and asked, "Like what?"

Paul put on his Cheshire Cat smile and vaguely answered, "Just because I couldn't directly contact you, I had other ways to talk to you. On the television, the grocery store, the radio…you know the usual advertisement spots."

It all came to Emily in a flash; everywhere she went, there was consistently an ad for his "practice" playing on the radio. In the background, while avoiding the truth, Paul was always there to entice her to seek "help."

"Sometimes, people don't understand. Sometimes it's hard to talk to others. And sometimes, we all just need a little help. That's where I can assist you." That ad was always around. Paul was a guardian of a sort in his way by manipulating analog and digital media.

"Why did I not know? How could I have not realized that I passed?" Emily asked, with tears forming in her eyes again.

Two figures emerged from the grey to greet Emily as she asked a fundamental question. A couple of her closest peers at Marie-Glen Elementary had died as well, and to add fuel to the proverbial fire, that was the truth. It was a pair she thought still lived. Margie Furlong, the next-door classroom neighbor, did not survive the blast to her chest when she diligently distracted the shooter so the children could run outside of the school. Margie also thought she hadn't died and thought the children, both dead and alive, were haunting her. Margie

Jamison Harris, the second-grade teacher, was one of the first casualties. His class was targeted by the shooter simply because he left the door open to keep the room cool. Fortunately, his students were in the gymnasium when the shots fired. When the perpetrator walked in with their shotgun, Jamison lifted his hands in the air and told him, "Not today," before most of his face was shot off by the mad man. When Jamison passed on, he was also one of the souls stranded on Earth, unable to tell Emily what had happened. Unlike the children, Jamison chose not to coax her with frights or convince her that she wasn't crazy for what she was seeing. Jamison just simply agreed and tried to be a friend. The rest of the time, he kept feeling his face to make sure that his looks were still intact and didn't resemble the after-effects of the shotgun blast. Even in death, people can always be vain.

Both Margie and Jamison walked out of the shadows to greet Emily. "Your last thought, the last thing you saw was red hitting your student's body. You assumed it was blood immediately, but it was just paint," Margie said, "You lived, sort to speak, with that thought, that idea…, that memory after you died and assumed it was the truth. She didn't die. You did. You just didn't know." Margie shrugged her shoulders as her eyes filled with tears again. Jamison put his arm around Margie to comfort her. It broke her heart to see Emily coming to the realization that she had passed.

Emily ran up to them both and embraced them. "I am so sorry this happened to you," Emily said as she fought back the tears.

"It's fine," Jamison replied. The presence of Emily comforted him. Even though Jamison would never have her love as he fantasized about in life, at least they could still be friends, even in death.

"It is?" Emily asked.

"Well, no, but in the end, we probably took the place of dozens of kids. That may have made a difference, don't you think? Maybe one of them will make a tire that doesn't deflate. I mean, it probably already has, and we just keep on paying for more to keep "the man" affluent."

"Here we go," Margie sighed, "It doesn't even matter for you anymore! Why are you getting worked up? You died!"

"Listen," Jamison intervened, "If we can take a rocket ship through a hot atmosphere, you mean to tell me that we can't make a tire that doesn't get a nail stuck in it at least!"

Emily chuckled to herself. It was like old times again. It and that was a small but welcome, slight relief to smile again, if only for a moment.

"Don't beat yourself up too much, girlie.," Margie insisted, "I swore that the kids were right behind me and that the shots may have hit one or two of them. I convinced myself that one of mine had died because I didn't react fast enough. It was only when Paul showed me the truth that I knew that they were way behind me."

Taking a step back from one another, they all looked at one another in silence. Paul walked toward them, waiting for the moment he could take them to their new home, their new life.

Jamison swayed back and forth. He mustered the courage to ask the question that Emily and Margie were also wondering. "So," Jamison started, "What now?"

Paul started to develop a blue aura around himself as he began to take Emily's and Jamison's hands. "That is a loaded question," Paul said with a sly smile. He wasn't going to answer him because surprises were much more fun. Not that Emily knew for sure, but she figured that laying out the overall journey was something that Paul's kind didn't do.

"I can't yet," Emily thought.

Paul whipped his head toward her as if he heard her thoughts. "What is it?" he asked Emily.

Emily spoke very quietly and said, "There is one last thing I need to do." She didn't want to explain herself, but Paul knew the closure concept and sympathized with it.

Paul let go of Emily's hand and took Margie's instead. He began to step back from Emily as Jamison and Margie followed him. The ground around them turned white as clouds started to form under their feet. Green particles emerged from the shadows, engulfing the three of them as orange and pink lights glistened, illuminating them. "Just remember," Paul said, "They will see you, and others may not, but they don't have to hear you for them to understand the message."

They began to disappear into the beautiful lights and particles. Margie smiled at her and, with her right hand, waved to Emily. Jamison nervously smiled at her and shrugged his shoulders, indicating that he had no idea where they were going. It was more to get one last laugh from Emily before they left the world they once knew forever. Emily put her hand on her lips and blew them a kiss before they dissipated into the light.

After taking a moment to compose herself and coming more to terms with what she had just learned about her fate, there was one thing that Emily realized. It wasn't the epiphany of what the children represented as "The Pales" and "The Dim" and how she interpreted them in her mind. It wasn't that the people around her weren't ignoring her; they simply couldn't see her. Those things would come to her overtime in her new life.

Emily realized then that her kids had broken into her apartment, terrifying the hell out of her. *Not just once, but at least a couple of times.* She couldn't be mad at them. They were trying to understand and help in their way—all of them. For Emily, that was the most significant achievement her students could have ever pulled off, human empathy.

It still scared me, though—those little ankle-biters.

<u>These Small Hearts</u>

After the clouds under her feet began to fade away, the rest of her surroundings began to retake shape. She was in an empty hallway—the hallway outside of her old classroom again. It was silent, a little too quiet for her comfort. Emily couldn't recall a time when her class was utterly speechless. Emily felt the dread again.

Paul finally revealed it all to her, and she still had the feeling in the pit of her stomach that something was wrong. She lightly stepped toward her old classroom, trying not to make any noise. Emily then realized that she couldn't make much noise, being that she was in an ethereal plane where she would be considered a spirit. Instead, she decided to just saunter to the door with her hands clasped together.

Peeking around the door, she could see her students. They were all there with their pure souls still in their precious little bodies with their small hearts. She had a sudden temptation to go inside and kiss them on the head started to overtake her thoughts. She realized that they probably would not feel it, at least not in the way she wanted. Emily emerged from the side of the door where anyone living could usually see her. Every child had their head buried in the assignment that given by the new teacher, *that new teacher*.

Watching the new teacher behind what was once her desk made Emily want to feel jealous and a bit nauseous for once. All the tiny imperfections in the wood were all too familiar to Emily. She glided her hand against the surface multiple times over the days she taught. She would never get to feel the dents and cracks ever again now.

The pretty redhead in her chair looked like she had just graduated high school, not college, and didn't dress appropriately for elementary, in Emily's opinion. She was sure that the young boys appreciated the short skirt with a bra that pushed up her breasts to her chin. To be fair, she was covered up modestly with pantyhose underneath her red plaid skirt, and her top buttoned appropriately. Emily looked at the whiteboard behind her and saw the name of Ms. Phoebe. *"Surely that was not her last name,"* Emily thought while rolling her eyes. *Wait. A whiteboard? They must have decided to upgrade.* It was a little irritating that she requested a whiteboard all the time she taught, and her room then gets one after she leaves. That was life on Earth, always moving on, allowing others to live and thrive the best they can.

The sound of gunfire rang through Emily's head suddenly as she pictured that day again with the sound of shotgun pellets penetrating the blackboard she once wrote on. She then remembered that she didn't just leave, she died, and life was moving on without her. It was a hard pill to swallow, but Emily needed to move on and not make her kids remember events they didn't want. Emily raised her hand to wave goodbye. "See ya later," she said lightly. Emily took her hand and pressed her pointer and middle finger against her lips to blow her students a kiss goodbye. As she exhaled, creating a breeze that lightly traveled into the classroom and along the top of Derek Singletary's head, that talented child would eventually come out of his shell.

Derek's Singletary's head slowly rose from working on his paper. As he scanned the room around him, his eyes locked on Emily. His old teacher was shrouded in pink, orange, and purple colors on the bottom half of her body from his perspective. Her hair was floating in the air like she was underwater, *"like a mermaid,"* that Derek immediately thought of when he saw Emily. Something he never thought could be possible.

Derek started to hit Bo Gentry's arm repeatedly. Bo kept shoving his hand away as he was deep into the assignment given to the class. Instead of purposefully answering the questions wrong, he knew that he was getting all of them correct. "Bo!" Derek whispered, confused about what he was seeing outside his classroom, a woman who resembled their teacher. Bo finally caved in.

"What?" Bo asked, hissed in a low, annoyed voice to avoid getting in trouble with the teacher. He looked up and saw his new teacher playing on her cell phone, so he knew that he had not been caught. As Bo sighed in relief, Derek put his hand on Bo's head and moved his eyes towards Emily's presence. Bo put his hand over his mouth, trying not to yell, "Holy shit!" like he wanted to, but some of those words came out anyways through his hands that quieted them. Bo caught the attention of Ava Nauling and, in turn, made Sloane Chastain curious as well. Before they could look back at Bo, they all saw Emily near the door tilting her head, wondering if they could see her. One by one, the students started to notice Emily. The beams of light pierced through the blinds, making it hard to see their teacher and her beautiful presence as the dust lingered in the air. It was almost time for Emily to go as she was between worlds and needed to leave this Earth.

Ava's mouth began to quiver as she attempted to fight back the tears that shortly overcame her. She caught her breath and composed herself to keep from being noticed, but that didn't stop the tears from flowing. As Ava cried, Sloane Chastain smiled at Emily and then looked at Brad as he whispered, "I told you it was her!" They knew the whole time, and none of them ever doubted it. That's the gift of being a child, the ability to believe in something so wholeheartedly while "rational" adults would scoff. People would give anything to feel like that again. All her children, even after her death, still believed in her.

Jamie Renee was the last to notice, but in a way, she was the first to feel a presence. Startled by her savior's appearance, Jamie's eyes began to fill with tears. Big alligator tears began to stream down her face.

All the children had seen her already after October 15th, but not like this. Not with a beautiful amalgamation of colors surrounding her. It was refreshing to see her beautiful again, not with the veil of darkness around her. When they encountered her in the streets or in her home before, Emily's students saw her the same way she saw Rachael McKay, sad and decomposing. If Paul had not made her know the truth, her soul could have ended up the same as Rachael's.

Emily was relieved to see them as they were, and not with black, cloudy eyes. That was the difference between them. The kids that appeared randomly with darkness around them were her students. The other children were other students who died during the tragedy.

Emily wanted to communicate but didn't want to draw attention to herself or have the kids make a scene. The only way was to use the sign language she taught them.

Hopefully, they still remember.

Emily took her time and moved her hands slowly to make sure everyone could see every one of her kids.

She pointed to herself and put her left-hand flat with her pinky finger up against her chest. Her right hand came down onto her left in a chopping-like motion and then brought back up, slightly pointed upward.

"I'm all right." she signed.

Emily pointed to herself again and shaped her hand to make an "O." She then pointed upward to the sky with her middle finger. Then outward, touching her thumb, creating the letter "K."

I'm o.k.

The children nodded and stared. They all knew what she signed but had a hard time focusing as Emily would be as all they could see was the closest thing they would see to an angel for a long time. Emily wished she had more time to teach them more sign language as she desperately wanted to tell them more. While it would have been quite the story, she realized that it was not her place to tell them what happens when they pass on, nor would she probably be allowed. Not knowing the result, trusting in yourself, and that the people you care about will choose the right path in life is part of what faith is.

Emily had to go, wherever that maybe, but she was sure it was good. A force was starting to tug at her to come along. There was only one thing to say that would define everything that she wanted from them in life. She gently put her fingers from her right hand to her lips and brought them down onto the inside of her left hand. Emily let her sign linger for a moment because she knew that she would have to leave as soon as her hands came apart. Emily didn't know if she could cry anymore but would leave her classroom wanting to.

Jamie was the first to bring her hands out. As soon as one of the kids saw her, they followed form. Without watching one another, all of Emily Sinclair's students, the kids that were "impossible to teach," brought their pointer fingers up to their chins. It was a simple gesture, but one that meant the most sometimes; each child signed:

"I'll miss you."

Some of the children were bewildered as some smiled, a few began to weep, and as it turned out to Emily's surprise, she could cry as well, even in death. Emily waved goodbye as she floated away and started to dissipate. Her entire class watched her begin to fade away into the beams of light that glistened inside the classroom.

Jamie Renee didn't cry even though her tears continued to linger within her eyes. She sat up in her seat and walked to the classroom window, moaning toward Emily, attempting to get her attention one last time. As her new teacher tried to get her attention to go back to her seat, Jamie stood in class, looking out a window and watching Emily float away. Jamie Renee looked around her classroom. It was the same, but it didn't have as much darkness lingering about it as it did after October 15th. Jamie smiled and let her tears go as she signed, *"Thank you."*

In the aftermath, thousands of people in the surrounding Cincinnati area donated money to help the victims' families. As disconnected from their daughter as they were, Emily's parents gave thousands of dollars to the school. Emily's life insurance money fell to Crosby. Instead of keeping all of it, Crosby used it to buy Marie-Glen Elementary's new floors and lockers. That was the only complaint that Emily ever had about her school. *It looks like the 70's died in there, and the '80s did the best it could to keep the look relevant,* she would say. No one ever hated Emily Sinclair after the shooting. No one was ignoring her like Emily thought before she knew she had passed on. It was quite the opposite; she was a hero all over the country. It was not for protecting her students during the shooting, though. Instead, Emily was recognized for aiding a group of children from all walks of life, getting them to communicate with one another and their families, not just with words but also with sign language.

If Emily knew about all the press she had received, she would have been embarrassed. Later in the afterlife, she found out that her fiancé, Crosby, was consistently questioned and bothered by people, and the press, for several months.

It was hard enough to walk away from Emily the night before her death, but to talk about her consistently took its toll. All he wanted was to move on, but something was still missing, despite talking about Emily for a long time to others. Nothing was working. He could have left Cincinnati or Ohio in general, but he stayed because he felt like he had to.

2

It was close to a year later from the day Emily Sinclair was buried, and while most of the world had moved on, Crosby Fulton had not. Crosby sat on a bench on the grass in front of Emily's gravestone. All he could do was stare at the engraving on the tombstone that read, "There is an opportunity for kindness wherever there is a human being." It wasn't an original quote, but it was one that Emily liked. Her parents thought it encapsulated Emily and her ideals.

The trees encapsulated him with vivid autumn colors. It used to be his favorite time of year. Any excuse to put on a sweater and scarf under his black pea coat was remarkable for his beatnik look he was so proud of. More than that, it was the crisp air and the colors he loved the most, like most people. Not today, though, not exactly. While the day was chilly, the air felt stagnant; no breeze came through, and the air smelled strange. The leaves started to fall, and in a rare event, orange leaves covered the ground as slivers of green grass poked through. The trees around the cemetery were also a sight to be seen. They were a light red as the foliage on the maple trees was about to fall soon.

Crosby didn't do much of anything anymore as he just existed in this world for the last year. He knew he had to go do something, or at least try. There was a bit of irony in his life without Emily; Crosby always wanted to go out and have a social life with Emily. He was very introverted most times, and without her, it didn't seem as important anymore. He wasn't sure if it was from sadness or maybe realizing that some things don't matter. Maybe both.

The last time Emily and Crosby spoke, their words were used as weapons to point out each other's faults. He wanted more in his life, and she wanted contentment. It ended with him walking out of the apartment they shared with a snide remark as Crosby left so that he could get in the last word; it was petty. Crosby didn't know why he did that; he hated people who felt they needed the last word to make an impact, no matter how inane it was.

The crunching of leaves behind Crosby grabbed his attention. Crosby looked behind him with an overpriced coffee in his hand. He looked around for someone, anybody for that matter; just some interaction would do. He was alone with his thoughts, and that was not the best place to be. Even though the afternoon started to cool, Crosby felt a warmth next to him suddenly.

Words started to enter his mind. It wasn't Crosby thinking hard or a conversation with someone he didn't know. It was the sound of Emily's voice; he knew that sound anywhere. As much as he wanted to walk away, he knew nothing left to lose from listening despite the possibility that he may be losing his mind.

"*Hey, my pretty man,*" he heard Emily's voice say, "*I need to say something to you.*"

3

As important as it was to say goodbye to her students in that final moment before she had to leave into her new existence, Emily knew that Crosby was a tortured soul. He was not dealing with her death well as everywhere he turned, there was a constant reminder. She needed to put some closure in his mind even though he was not able to see her. It was rare for someone that had died to come back to Earth to tie up loose ends. Most embrace their new life, so to speak, and forget about their troubles. Emily was not like most people. She wanted to make sure people who were part of her life were going to be excellent for the rest of their lives in a meaningful way in death and life. Crosby was the only one that wasn't coping.

She walked behind him as he sat on the bench near her gravesite. It was a bit surreal for Emily to see her gravestone. For a moment, she had a narcissistic question: *I wonder how many people showed up to my funeral*, the question that many wonder about in life as they ponder their death. Crosby sat on the right side of the bench, placing his elbow on the arm as he rested his face on his hands. Emily noticed how much paler he had become and the dark circles under his eyes from the lack of good sleep. Emily sat down next to her love with her white, heavenly dress flowing in the wind, trying not to make a sound. She did not know if she could interact with objects, but the crumbling leaves grabbed Crosby's attention.

He looked straight at Emily as she paused, wondering if Crosby could see her form. After what seemed to be minutes, Crosby turned back around to drift off with his thoughts. Emily sighed and sat next to him on the bench. She secretly wanted him to see her one more time, but deep down, she knew that it might do more harm than good. Any progress Crosby had made in the grieving process could fall to pieces if he saw her again.

Before she began to speak, she looked at the splendor that an autumn day in the Midwest looked and maybe felt like; Emily wasn't sure how cold it was because she couldn't feel it on her skin, not anymore. She missed it.

Emily wasn't sure what to say. What could she say? Should she apologize for not haunting him earlier? Maybe tell him that everything was going to be all right? It was the last time she was allowed on Earth, and she needed to make it count.

"Hey, my pretty man," Emily said again as he loved hearing it when they were together, "I need to say something to you."

4

"I need to say I'm sorry to you," Emily started, "I don't care who was right or even who was wrong. The truth is that no one was the winner in the end, and I think I was spiteful toward you because of my own issues in life, and that's not fair to you."

Crosby's eyes opened wider as he wasn't sure if he was making up this one-sided conversation in his mind. Instead of instinctively retorting in case anyone was watching, he let it play out.

"I said you were a child. I said you were weak, and I told you to grow up and live in the real world. I tried to take down your dreams and aspirations in a single moment to have the gratification of taking you down mentally to prove a point selfishly." Emily began to cry. "I knowingly tried to punch you in the heart as hard as possible and not look back at that moment. I said things to you that I feel shameful, and I don't understand why I am not being punished for it."

Crosby put his hand over his mouth, and with closed eyes, he mumbled, "Don't. Please don't." His body convulsed a bit as he choked back his sorrow so no one would see it. His nose ran, and his throat began to dry as the air he refused to release eventually exuded in the form of a whimper. No one was around, but he still refused to let loose his pain and sorrow.

Emily put her hand up to tell him not to speak but forgot she couldn't. Crosby didn't say another word because he thought her voice had gone away.

It was hard to get the words out, but. Emily sobbed heavily for a moment but composed herself as she knew that her time was limited.

"The fact is that you are the most real, the bravest person I know. So brave. Even with the cards being dealt against you, you don't cave and move on. You know who you are, and you never apologized for it, no matter what others thought about it. You are my feisty man with a heart of gold even though others may not see it as I did...like I do."

"Please stop," he pleaded with Emily's voice, "You can't do this now. There's nothing in me anymore. It's all gone. I have nothing left inside."

Emily shook her head in disagreement as her tears flew from her face into the air, where they turned into sparkling light that quickly disappeared.

"I don't believe that," she said sternly, "You have so much more to give to the world, and if there is only a single person that knows what you have in you, then that's enough. It shouldn't be about the many. Maybe the few are the ones that matter most. I believe that more people will realize the wonderful person you are as time goes on. I said that I envied my students because they still had a chance in life that you didn't have anymore; I was wrong. You were living that chance that life when I was with you, and I didn't realize it."

Emily began to think about all the good in her former life, dancing around the apartment together, getting a piggyback ride through the grocery store. The moment he wrote a song for her and performed it live on stage. It was almost overwhelming, but she didn't know that Crosby was running through a set of memories of his own, some the same but others she would never know. Watching her when she wasn't aware, basking in everything that made Emily a person, those things only he was able to see and appreciate. Crosby remembered the first times when he touched Emily's skin or brushed her hair away from her face as she slept so she wouldn't choke. She put her hands to his face and placed them onto his cheeks. Crosby could barely feel it, and neither could Emily, but it was enough for her to know she tried. Emily kissed his head and said, "But you have to go on …it's okay. Don't worry about me. Be happy; however, you can, because it's the only thing you can do in this life that matters most."

Emily put her head on his shoulder as she started to disappear. "What am I supposed to do without you?" Crosby cried.

Emily stared off into the beauty of the fall leaves and replied, "I don't know. I can't answer that. You gotta figure that one out yourself, kiddo. That's life, though, I suppose." It's hard to say goodbye to someone, but it's harder to let go.

Crosby slightly smiled with a stream of tears staining his face. As Emily's body began to dissipate, Crosby could feel the warmth fading away. In the final moments, before she went back to her new home, Crosby turned his head and saw Emily's spirit smile. His muscles in his mouth began to burn from holding back weeping. Crosby told Emily what he should have said a long time ago: she told him,

"What else can I say? You are my best friend. No matter what I do in life, you will always be the best part about it."

The End

Final Author Thoughts

Well, that only took three years to get through the first draft. While I know it may not seem like much, especially if you can read an entire book in a day, this was the most challenging book I have ever written up to this point. The idea of writing a horror story based on real events was one thing. Those are now considered a regular occurrence. Then, trying to spin it into something positive used up much imagination. It was emotionally exhausting.

For those who have, or will ask, the inevitable question, "Why didn't we read about what the shooter looked like, or their name?" the answer is simple--it doesn't matter. It doesn't matter if it was a man or a woman, white or black, Christian or Islamic; the act is that of a monster. Aren't the scariest monsters the ones we can hardly see?

Small Hearts is a story about the people that died and those that survived, albeit they are fictional people. Still, it relates to the times we are currently enduring. I sometimes wonder what happens in our schools and communities' real heroes' minds when the shooting starts. What would I do? Would we care so much about the evil that started the chain of events if we knew more about the victims and heroes? Like Victoria Soto, a first-grade teacher from Sandy Hook Elementary, died saving her students. We'll never know, but it can't all be for nothing. If there aren't as many heroes as there are villains, then what the hell is the point of this world we live in?

Other Works from Bryan W. Dull

Solstice

Equinox

Ecliptic

Celestial

Pill Hill

Shorts

Daddy

Sewer Drains & Lighthouses

Christian's Christmas Conundrum

About the Author

Bryan W. Dull writes books, which, if you really knew him, makes perfect sense as that's all he has done since sixth grade, spinning a yarn at a moment's notice. He is best known for writing horror and suspense stories. Solstice was his first novel and foray into publishing (it was a bet to do it, by the way). In 2016, he tried his hand at something different and published a personal story, Pill Hill. Now, Bryan W. Dull is becoming known for being a literary voice of hope…with some scares mixed into it occasionally. He lives in Fort Wayne, IN, with his wife and daughter and plans on writing more stories that have something to say in this strange world that we live in.